HUNTING THE HUNTER

GORDON KORMAN TAKES YOU TO THE EDGE OF ADVENTURE

ON THE RUN

DIVE

EVEREST

ISLAND

www.SCHOLASTIC.com

www.GORDONKORMAN.com

GORDON KORMAN

ON THE RUN

CHASE #6

HUNTING THE HUNTER

AN
APPLE
PAPERBACK

SCHOLASTIC INC.

New York   Toronto   London   Auckland   Sydney
Mexico City   New Delhi   Hong Kong   Buenos Aires

No part of this publication may be reproduced, stored in a retrieval system, or transmitted in any form or by any means, electronic, mechanical, photocopying, recording, or otherwise, without written permission of the publisher. For information regarding permission, write to Scholastic Inc., Attention: Permissions Department, 557 Broadway, New York, NY 10012.

ISBN 0-439-65141-7

12 11 10 9 8 7 6 5 4   6 7 8 9 10 11/0

Printed in the U.S.A.   40

First printing, February 2006

For David Levithan,
who gives *On the Run* its legs

Aiden Falconer was milking cows again.

He had come full circle. This nightmare had begun at a juvenile prison farm in Nebraska. That was where he and his sister, Meg, had been sent after their parents had been convicted of treason and locked away for life.

Back then they had been inmates, prisoners — before the fire, the escape. Now they were fugitives, wanted by the FBI, the juvenile authorities, and dozens of state and local police forces.

But the cows — they were the same. Uncooperative, cranky, and with a stink that would choke a sewer rat.

Everybody else could milk a cow. Meg could fill a bucket in no time. Why was it that every cow shut down milk production as soon as it sensed Aiden's fear?

It shouldn't take a PhD to do this!

That started a new train of thought, a much more

unpleasant one. Mom and Dad both had PhD's. And their expertise had been used to frame them and destroy the Falconer family.

The lapse in concentration cost him. The cow lifted its rear hoof and delivered a hammer blow to Aiden's stomach. The wallop sent him off the stool and into the soft straw.

In despair, Aiden gathered his gear and steeled himself for another attempt.

There was a purpose to all this, he reminded himself. This job as a farmhand — it wasn't a career move; it was a hiding place. For Aiden and Meg to show their faces in Denver right now would be to risk instant arrest. But on this farm, just twenty miles east of the city limits, they could disappear for a while, with Aiden posing as the hired worker and Meg keeping out of sight. They could lie low until the heat was off and prepare themselves for the awful thing they had to do.

Six big cows, one piddly little bucket of milk. How was he going to explain that to Mr. Turnbull? The farmer had a broken leg, not brain damage. How long before it dawned on the man that his "experienced" hired hand was a suburban fifteen-year-old who didn't know the difference between a cow and third base?

The next order of business was taking the herd out to pasture. It was a slightly more pleasant task. He still had to deal with the cows, but at least the paralyzing stench of the barn could be left behind for a few minutes before shoveling time.

God, I hate farming!

The collision came from behind. It was so powerful, so devastating, his first thought was that he'd been hit by a car. The impact knocked the air out of him, propelling him six feet forward. Then his attacker was upon him, three hundred pounds of rooting, snarling rage.

He had seen the pig from a distance. It was the size of a Volkswagen, easily four times bigger than the other pigs in the sty. Hooves like sledgehammers pounded down at him. The huge drooling snout battered him about the head and face. Aiden struggled, but the crushing weight pressed down on his rib cage.

The thought was as horrifying as it was absurd: *This animal is killing me!*

He had escaped manhunts covering thousands of miles. He had survived murder attempts and life-and-death struggles. Was he really going to die here in this pasture, cut down by an enraged swine?

Wham!

The flat of the shovel connected with the pig's hindquarters in a home-run swing. With a squeal of shock, the beast rolled off Aiden and squared off against eleven-year-old Meg Falconer, an attacker barely a quarter of its weight.

Aiden leaped to his feet, muddy and bleeding, his clothes torn. "Meg — run!"

But his sister faced the danger like a gladiator, brandishing her shovel. "Don't even think about it, Porko, or you'll be bacon bits before you can say *oink*!"

Aiden watched, amazed, as the giant animal backed off, whining like a whipped puppy. The other spectators, the cows, looked on, chewing disinterestedly.

"What are you doing out here?" Aiden hissed. "If Mr. Turnbull sees you, how long do you think it's going to take him to figure out who we really are?"

"What was I supposed to do — hide in the loft and let this thing crush you? Fat lot of good it'll do Mom and Dad if one of us gets killed."

That was the goal of these weeks on the run — to prove that their parents were innocent of treason. They had finally tracked down the man who had framed Doctors John and Louise Falconer, only to find that he was a vicious killer. It was the end of one problem and the beginning of an even bigger one — how could two kids capture a professional assassin?

Meekly, the pig backed away and trotted off in the direction of the sty.

Around the corner of the barn, the farmhouse's screen door creaked open, then slapped shut.

"Scram!" Aiden whispered urgently.

Meg beat a hasty retreat into the barn and up the ladder to the hayloft.

Aiden didn't add, "Thanks for saving my life." Over the past weeks, both Falconers had rescued each other so often that one more time didn't bear mentioning.

We're turning into hard cases, a couple of action heroes who don't think a brush with death is worth a thank-you.

Meg needn't have rushed into hiding, because it took a long time for Zephraim Turnbull to thump his way on his crutches out to the pasture and his bleeding hired hand.

Mr. Turnbull looked like every picture Aiden had ever seen of a leather-faced American farmer — stoic, weather-beaten, and humorless.

"I see you've met old Bernard," the farmer observed drily. "Suppose I should have warned you about him. Nasty piece of work."

Aiden brushed at his sleeve, which removed about one percent of the mud that covered him. "I can take care of myself," he said defensively.

Turnbull looked him up and down. "I can see that. You sure you're eighteen?"

Aiden straightened, setting aside his many aches and pains. "Absolutely. I'm just trying to make some extra money for when I start college in January."

"Suppose I can't fault you for not being ready for Bernard," the farmer decided grudgingly. "He comes on pretty strong, but that's why I keep him around."

"You mean he's a guard pig?"

Turnbull nodded. "You can't be too careful with Holyfield and his lawyers nosing around."

It had all been explained to Aiden the day Turnbull had hired him: Mountain View Homes, the land developer, owned every single property as far as the eye could see . . . except one. The Turnbull farm was not for sale.

Actually, it *was* for sale. But Turnbull still had seventeen years to go on his family's ninety-nine-year lease. And he didn't intend to be begged or bribed off his farm.

"I guess Mr. Holyfield wants to sell pretty bad, huh?" Aiden said.

Turnbull nodded. "You should have seen his face when he found out I was in a cast for six weeks. If the land isn't farmed, the lease is null and void. That's where you come in. A good, experienced hand to tide me over until I'm on my feet again." He regarded Aiden dubiously. "Eighteen, huh? Well, follow me. We'll have to get those cuts cleaned up. That's a lot more than mud, you know, with all these animals around."

The farmer thumped his way back to the house with Aiden trailing along behind him. As he stepped up to the wooden porch, his foot nudged something metal, knocking it off the platform to the grass. The loud report that reached Aiden's ears needed no identification.

It was a gunshot.

 2

Life on the run had sharpened Aiden's response time. He hit the dirt before the echo died and rolled under the porch.

When Zephraim Turnbull turned to investigate the source of the noise, his hired man had disappeared.

"You okay, Gary?" he asked. Gary Graham was Aiden's alias.

"Get down!" Aiden hissed. He was absolutely convinced that Frank Lindenauer, the man who had framed their parents, was shooting at him from cover. Five days before, Aiden and Meg had barely escaped him in a Denver cemetery.

Meg — Aiden thought of his sister, hidden away in the barn, completely unprotected. How could he reach her without making himself an easy target?

"My fault. Sorry," came the voice of Zephraim

Turnbull. "It's just a nail gun. Shouldn't leave it lying around."

Pale and shaking, Aiden emerged from the shadows under the porch. Not Frank Lindenauer. Not this time. "A nail gun?" he repeated in a daze.

Turnbull nodded. "I'm replacing some of these rotted planks." He flashed Aiden a satisfied grimace. "That'll show Holyfield I'm not planning to go anywhere. If he wants this farm, he can have it — in seventeen years."

Aiden picked up the device and handed it to the farmer, who rested it on the porch rail. That explained the percussive cracks that reached the Falconers in the farmhand's apartment attached to the barn. They had been awakening each dawn to what sounded like a gunfight.

Aiden stood patiently on the porch while Turnbull washed his face and painted his cuts with dark orange iodine. "Don't trust those newfangled ointments," his employer said flatly. "The old ways are the best. Wouldn't be using that blasted nail gun, but my bum leg makes it hard to get squared up to swing a hammer."

The front door was open, and Aiden could see inside. The house was very much like its occupant —

simple, harsh, and spare. Much of the furniture was unpainted wood, and even the upholstered living room couch had a severe, sit-up-straight quality to it. A brand-new computer, still in its factory packing, sat in an open box by the wall.

Turnbull noticed Aiden's interest in the Dell system. "From my nephew in New York City last Christmas," he explained. "He figured we could stay in touch through e-mail."

"You haven't taken it out of the box yet," Aiden observed.

"You got that right."

All at once, there was a loud squealing noise, and Bernard stampeded past, an enraged pig closer in size to a buffalo. Hooves thundering, he scrambled around the corner of the house and charged down the dirt drive.

A few seconds later, a car door slammed, and a gray sedan screeched away from the farm and out of sight, burning rubber.

The incident produced the closest thing to a smile Aiden had yet seen on his employer's lips. "Show me a private investigator with the belly to tangle with Bernard, and I'll show you a man without fear."

Aiden didn't share the farmer's good humor. Weeks on the run had taught him that mysterious spies watching from a distance were nothing to joke about. Maybe it had been just a snoop hired by Holyfield to force Turnbull out.

Maybe.

But with Frank Lindenauer out there somewhere, and with hundreds of cops on the alert for the Falconer fugitives, a private investigator would be the least of Aiden's worries.

At six feet seven inches tall, FBI Agent Emmanuel Harris was an intimidating presence. Yet he could not intimidate the Denver office's coffeepot to percolate any faster. It bubbled and glubbed, taking its own sweet time, while Harris watched with his empty cup, glaring.

Slow-brewing coffee was not the cause of his foul mood. He had lost the Falconer kids again. This was nothing new. The young fugitives had been dodging him for weeks, appearing from thin air and then vanishing just as quickly. But never before had they remained out of sight for so long. Six days ago, Aiden and Margaret had eluded Harris, not to mention half the Denver police department. They had not been heard from since.

While waiting for the kids to resurface, Harris was reexamining their parents' court case — all nineteen thousand pages of it. The towers of paper barely fit inside the tiny converted closet he was using as an office here in Denver.

Doctors John and Louise Falconer — the respected criminology professors convicted of aiding and abetting foreign terrorists. The most notorious traitors in half a century. Only the longer Harris gave the documents a second look, the flimsier the case against the Falconers seemed to be. The professors were in prison not because of overwhelming evidence against them. They had been found guilty simply because they had been unable to produce one witness — a CIA agent named Frank Lindenauer.

The CIA insisted there was no such person.

"We should have looked harder," Harris mumbled aloud to the coffeepot. He was the agent who had "cracked" the Falconer case. It was *his* fault that Aiden and Margaret's parents were in maximum security. It was *his* fault that Aiden and Margaret were now fugitives.

The kids claimed to have found new evidence. They said Lindenauer not only existed, but he had framed their parents. Could that be true?

The pot had no opinion. It continued to percolate at its maddeningly slow pace.

"Hey, Harris —" A white-coated lab tech leaned in the doorway. "I knew I'd find you here. You spend more time in the coffee room than your office."

"What have you got for me?" Harris interrupted.

"Washington was able to lift a couple of partial fingerprints off the pistol they found at the cemetery. One print belonged to the girl — Margaret."

"And the other?" The second could only belong to the owner of the gun — "Hairless Joe," the mysterious bald killer who had been stalking the Falconers for thousands of miles.

"It's all right here." The lab tech handed over a file folder and disappeared down the hall.

Breathlessly, Harris opened the manila cover and examined the contents. *Terence J. McKenzie*. He frowned. The name didn't ring a bell.

According to the file, Terence J. McKenzie had been a low-level CIA operative, working in anti-terror. Back in 1995, his bosses had become nervous that he was becoming too friendly with the terrorist groups he was supposed to be investigating. But just when McKenzie was about to be fired, he disappeared. This fingerprint was the first sign of him in nearly a decade.

Harris turned the page. Pasted at the top of McKenzie's personnel record was a photograph of a young man with long, thick red hair and a full beard.

Harris gawked. He knew this face! He had seen it on the street posters that had been designed to trap the Falconer kids in Los Angeles. That man was Hairless Joe!

It all fit — Terence McKenzie had shaved his face and head in an attempt to elude his former colleagues in the CIA. He was the missing piece of this puzzle, the phantom who had eluded the powerful magnifying glass of the trial of the new millennium.

Terence McKenzie was the man John and Louise Falconer knew as Frank Lindenauer.

The Rocky Mountains were growing taller, lengthening from an uneven line of gravel along the flat horizon.

Zephraim Turnbull's pickup truck rattled west along County Road G-17, Aiden at the wheel. The farmer had given him forty bushel baskets of turnips to take to the Denver Produce Terminal. After a week of lying low in the country, the Falconers had decided to use the trip to test the waters. Seven days before, they had been front-page news in this city. Would they be able to move about without attracting attention from the public? And, more to the point, the police?

Meg was confused. "We're going to hawk turnips?"

Aiden laughed. "They're already sold. We just have to deliver them to the supermarket guys. Mr. Turnbull put me through Turnip 101 when I got the job."

Meg glanced dubiously out the back window at the payload. "It would take a lot to get me to eat one of those."

"Better to eat them than lift them. Those baskets weigh a ton." Aiden's body still ached from loading the truck.

The countryside was flat and boring, but Meg was surprised to find herself enjoying the ride. It was a crisp, clear day with a nip of fall in the air. When she closed her eyes, it was almost possible to imagine Mom and Dad waiting for them at home.

The vision clouded. Serving life sentences at his and hers maximum security prisons in Florida, Mom and Dad hadn't been waiting at home for more than a year.

No — don't think about that. . . .

Well, at least she was out of the barn. She'd spent most of the past week skulking in the Turnbull hayloft. Agriculture wasn't fun, but it gave Aiden something to do. She had taken over some of the milking duty because he was so hopeless at it. But at the first sign of the farmer, she'd had to run and hide. She was quietly losing her mind from the inactivity.

To loll around with a bunch of cows, killing time

while the days turn into weeks, while Mom and Dad are suffering in prison....

She could imagine no greater torture.

Denver Produce Terminal was like a city in itself, a vast, bustling farmers' market. Meg had never seen so many trucks in her life. Workers swarmed around them like armies of ants. The sound was a symphony of urgent shouts, mingling together into a babble that assaulted the ears. It was pure chaos, yet there was an underlying order to it. Food shipments arrived; their cargoes were unloaded. It all happened somehow.

A hard-hatted foreman waved Aiden in through the gate.

He regarded his sister. "Ready?"

She adjusted her sunglasses. "Let's go."

If the Falconers were about to be identified . . . if the pointing fingers and cries of recognition were about to fly . . . if 9-1-1 was about to be dialed, it would surely happen in the next few minutes.

Meg had dyed her hair dark brown and cut it razor-short. The new appearance didn't thrill her, but it made a lot of sense. Her most recent pictures in the media showed a blond girl, not a brunette boy. There wasn't a whole lot Aiden could do to disguise himself. A complete makeover would be suspicious to Mr. Turnbull. Still, the sight of two boys was very different from a boy and a girl.

Besides, nobody looks for fugitives in Veggie Land. Zucchini, maybe, but not fugitives.

Meg noticed a trickle of sweat on Aiden's brow as he labored to maneuver the pickup through the close quarters of workers and stalls and other vehicles. The slightest mishap or fender bender could lead to talk of insurance and a driver's license — and the fact that Aiden didn't have either. He had taught himself to drive because he'd had no choice. More than once, a car, motorcycle, or ATV had been their only means of escape.

This is the first time we've ever driven something we didn't have to steal.

The fresh produce was being unloaded from the trucks into endless rows of connected warehouses. These ranged in size from large storage lockers to the massive complex run by Great West Supermarkets, the Turnbull farm's number-one customer.

While Aiden helped the Great West people unload the pickup, Meg tried to lie low. It was impossible. The produce terminal was too crowded, and an eleven-year-old stood out in this adult workplace. The probing eyes produced a fear in her that penetrated her soul. She was not easily recognizable as Margaret Falconer. But she could tell from the frowns and furrowed brows that her features were familiar to people. They knew her from somewhere; they just couldn't place it.

And if one of them figures out there's a twenty-five-thousand-dollar reward on my head —

A hand grabbed her shoulder, and she practically jumped out of her skin.

"It's just me," Aiden soothed.

"Let's beat it," she urged. "I've been getting weird looks left, right, and center. It's only a matter of time before somebody puts a name to the face."

"If we keep on hiding, we'll never be able to make our move on Hairless Joe," her brother countered.

The mysterious bald assassin had been hunting them since Vermont. It had taken a lot of terrifying near misses before they had realized that Hairless Joe was none other than Frank Lindenauer.

"We don't have a move," she pointed out bitterly. "Up till a week ago, we didn't even know that Hairless Joe was really Hairless Frank. He was just the big cueball who was shooting at us. What makes you think we can go anywhere near him now?"

Aiden dropped his voice to a whisper. "I might know a place where we could set a trap for him."

Meg pounced on this. Capturing Lindenauer was the only way to prove their parents' innocence.

"Where?"

"Here."

"Are you nuts?" she hissed. "In this madhouse?"

"It's only a madhouse during work hours," Aiden argued. "At night, it's probably deserted. Look —" He indicated a few rows of older, shabbier storage units on the far west side of the facility. No trucks were parked in this area; no workers swarmed busily around.

Meg squinted after his pointing finger. "I guess they stopped using the old section when these newer warehouses went up."

He led her around a parked forklift to a small rise where they had a better view of the abandoned structures. They were about the size of single-car garages and could be secured by means of pull-down metal gates. "If we can convince Hairless Frank to meet us in one of those units, maybe we can lock him into it."

It was a measure of not just their daring but also their desperation that Meg didn't even question the wisdom of such a dangerous plan. "But how do we get in touch with him? We don't have his address or his phone number, and Frank Lindenauer is probably a phony name. It's not like we can take out an ad in the paper for a murderer and hope that he answers."

Aiden looked surprised, then impressed. "Meg, you're a genius."

She was horrified. "I'm *kidding*!"

"But I'm not."

UNCLE FRANK — We have to stop fighting before somebody gets hurt. Let's meet and come to an agreement. E-mail us at <u>falx@zipnet.usa.</u> Your loving nephew and niece, A & M.

Meg looked up from the paper. "We don't have an e-mail address."

"Yeah, but Mr. Turnbull has a brand-new computer, still in the box," Aiden explained. "I'll volunteer to put it together for him. And while I'm setting up his e-mail account, I can sneak in a secret address for us. The guy hates technology — he'll never know the difference."

The two sat in the pickup's cab in the parking lot of the *Denver Chronicle*, poring over the text of the personal ad they hoped would lead them to their deadly enemy.

His sister was unconvinced. "You really think he'll answer this?"

"He'll have to. He wants to find us as much as we want to find him. He's probably tearing the city apart for us right now."

The thought was far from comforting. Frank Lindenauer was a cold-blooded killer, ruthless and efficient.

Aiden swallowed hard and went on. "*Uncle Frank* — that's what I used to call him back when I was six, when he was Mom and Dad's friend."

"*Friend!*" Meg practically spat the word. "He ruined our lives, and he did it to help terrorists. He doesn't know the meaning of the word."

"The point is, he'll know it has to be from us," Aiden insisted. "Let's just hope he reads newspapers."

"Maybe we should put the ad in *Killers' Home Journal*."

It sounded like a joke; it was nothing of the kind. Aiden and Meg had spent the last few weeks *fleeing* from this man. Seeking him out on purpose screamed of pure insanity.

If there was another way . . . Aiden thought.

But there wasn't. Any future for the Falconer

family lay in this lethal game of cat and mouse. They had to capture this traitor before he could destroy them.

Meg stayed in the truck while Aiden entered the *Chronicle* building to place the ad. It was one thing to be seen together at the produce terminal. But this was one of the many newspapers that had reported the flight of the young fugitives to the world. Aiden navigated the labyrinth of hallways, fighting to control the jitters in his heart. He felt like a trainer with his head inside the jaws of a fierce lion — a front-page story marching through the offices of a hungry news organization.

Personal Ads was on the main floor, in the far corner behind the employee cafeteria. The office reminded Aiden of a classroom, with a large desk up front and smaller workstations where customers could compose their ads. His hopes of blending in with the crowd were dashed immediately. *He* was the crowd, except for the clerk in charge.

The young woman noticed his surprise at the empty office. "These days, most of our stuff comes in over the Internet," she explained.

Aiden nodded nervously. He would have greatly preferred to do the same, but without a credit card, he had no choice but to present himself in person.

He handed over the paper with the carefully worded ad. "How much would this cost?"

At lightning speed, she keyboarded the message. "Four lines at fourteen-fifty per line — fifty-eight dollars. That runs it for five days."

"Fine," Aiden replied, placing three twenties on the counter. "Will it start tomorrow?"

"In the afternoon paper," she told him. "The morning edition is already set." She struck a key to send the ad to Composing. "Have you been in here before? You seem familiar."

The question struck him like a body blow. "Not me," he managed to reply. "This is my first time."

"Funny," she mused. "I'm really good with faces."

He looked away quickly and caught a startling glimpse of why his appearance rang a bell with her. The office was decorated with mounted *Chronicle* front pages. One of them, positioned almost directly in front of the clerk's desk, featured two sickeningly familiar photographs. They were the mug shots of Aiden and Margaret Falconer from the Department of Juvenile Corrections.

In a panic, Aiden could feel his lunch rising. "Am I all done?" He was already striding through the door, his mind intent on escape.

"Wait!" she exclaimed suddenly.

It took a superhuman effort not to break into a sprint for the front exit, the pickup truck, and a speedy getaway.

He turned in the doorway, ready to argue, deny, and when all else failed, to run.

She was standing up, holding her hand out to him. "You forgot your change."

"Oh, right," he wheezed. "Thanks."

He accepted the bills, wheeled, and fled.

In the parking lot, Meg regarded him in alarm. "What happened? You're all white."

That was life balanced on a knife edge. Even when nothing went wrong, it was still a major frightfest.

Zephraim Turnbull was unimpressed by the computer that sat on a card table in his living room. When Aiden showed him the finished product, his pronouncement was: "It's not necessary."

"But you can order feed and grain online," Aiden argued. "And look — this Web site tracks the price of turnips in Chicago trading."

"If it can't keep Holyfield's goons from sticking their noses into my business, then it's as useful as udders on a bull," the farmer decided.

Aiden wasn't sure whether or not to believe that the property was under surveillance by its landowner. He had seen no spies himself. Every now and then, Bernard would thunder off on a snarling rampage after something or other. But the watch pig did that every time the mail carrier tried to tiptoe up to the box.

"You can't go by a wild beast," was his opinion, shared with Meg later on in the barn.

"He's not wild," Meg retorted. "He's just doing his job guarding the farm."

Didn't it figure? Bernard, who hated everybody, had chosen Meg to love. Ever since that shovel in the behind, the pig had been hanging around the barn, scaring the cows, and following Meg like an adoring puppy — or at least a baby elephant.

"You're not safe with that thing," Aiden warned her. "It's a prehistoric mammal."

The pig shot him a baleful look as it presented its huge snout for Meg to pat.

The good news was that Zephraim Turnbull was encouraging Aiden to try out the computer because "someone should get use out of that chrome-plated whatchamagizmo." Several times each day, Aiden interrupted his chores to access the secret e-mail account. So far, there had been no response to the *Chronicle* ad.

It had been only a day and a half since the personal had first appeared, but Aiden was already nervous. What if their message never reached Frank Lindenauer? He racked his brain for other ways to get in touch with the assassin, but came up empty. That was the Falconers' greatest fear — not running into danger so much as running out of options.

It was after midnight when Aiden let himself into the residence and tiptoed to the computer in the living room. His employer had been asleep since nine. With the farmer's buzz-saw snores resounding throughout the small house, Aiden booted up the machine and opened the in-box for falx@zipnet.usa.

And there it was.

Dear A & M,
I feel the same way. Family shouldn't be fighting. It's time to let bygones be bygones. Let's arrange a meeting so we can bury the hatchet.
Your Uncle Frank

He sat frozen, staring at the monitor. The relief that flooded through him was tempered with apprehension. This was a message from Frank Lindenauer, their archenemy. It was just words on a screen, computer code traveling through the Internet. But the mere thought that this brutal assassin could reach them, even electronically, made him feel exposed and vulnerable.

Calm down, he commanded himself. *This is what you've been hoping for*.

With trembling fingers, he keyboarded a reply.

Uncle Frank — meet us at Denver Produce
Terminal, inside unit 129. Tomorrow night,
1 a.m.
See you there,
A & M

As he clicked the mouse to send the message,
Aiden wondered if he had just signed a death war-
rant for himself and his sister.

By the dim light from a sliver of moon, the door of the farmhand's apartment opened and two shadowy figures stole out into the darkness. They crossed the barnyard, heading for the old pickup truck parked on the dirt drive.

The hoofbeats came from the left — a steady rhythm, gaining in speed and percussion. Out of the gloom appeared Bernard in full flight, head down, ears flattened — a charging beast approaching ramming speed.

Aiden was frozen with fright. He stood rooted to the spot, waiting to be trampled.

Not Meg. She stepped out into the path of three hundred pounds of rampaging pork, threw up her hand like a traffic cop, and rasped, *"Hey!"*

Watching the huge creature putting on the brakes would have been comical if the whole thing hadn't been so scary. Trotters skittering, Bernard ground to a halt by dragging his immense bottom on the turf.

"It's just us," Meg whispered. "Go back to sleep."

Aiden watched in amazement as the monster pig turned and slunk off into the gloom.

"How do you *do* that?" he hissed as they let themselves into the pickup. "Cows love you, that thing hates everybody, and *he* loves you, too."

"They don't love me; they *respect* me. If you show fear to a bully like Bernard, he'll jump all over you."

Aiden kept his mouth shut. Fear of Bernard was not something he was likely to conquer any time soon.

The drive took only twenty minutes on deserted roads, so they were early. Denver Produce Terminal, once a vast beehive of activity, was dark and empty.

"It looks like an abandoned prisoner-of-war camp," Meg observed, surveying the sprawling expanse of wire fencing and buildings, but no people.

"Creepy," Aiden agreed. "But not half as creepy as the guy we're here to meet."

Meg bit her lip. Hanging around a commercial wasteland in the dead of night may have been scary. But that fear was a wisp of nothing compared with the prospect of facing down a professional killer in the flesh.

This is it, she thought. *Us against Frank Lindenauer.*

They drove off the main road and nestled the pickup behind a stand of trees. As they approached the front gate, Meg wished she had something darker to wear. When they'd purchased their thrift shop clothing, blending in had been their goal, not disappearing into the shadows of a big city food depot.

The gate was locked, but the property wasn't exactly impenetrable. They followed the fence until they found a gap between the ground and the chain mesh. Lean Meg had no problem slithering underneath. Aiden had a few anxious moments when a belt loop on his jeans got snagged on a link, but his sister managed to drag him through.

The terminal smelled of diesel fuel and rotting fruit. The only illumination came from mounted arc lights, like the ones used by night construction crews. These were located in the busier parts of the big facility. As they made their way toward the out-of-use area that contained Unit 129, it grew so dark that they could barely see their hands in front of their faces.

Aiden switched on a flashlight and played the beam over the rows of crumbling storage garages. No fuel-and-fruit aroma here; this was no longer a working part of the terminal. It had become a

dump. Broken bricks, siding, and roof shingles lit-
tered the tarmac. Nothing had been stored in any of
these units for a long time. Most of the security gates
were so bent, dented, and rusted that they probably
wouldn't have rolled up or down.

At last, the flashlight shone on a rusted metal
placard — 129. In this crumbling forgotten structure, Aiden and Meg would make their stand to win
justice for their poor parents.

Or die trying. Meg thought it but she didn't dare
say it aloud.

The plan was this: Lie in wait until Hairless
Frank entered the unit, then pull down the gate and
padlock the assassin inside. Next, call Agent Emmanuel Harris, to tell him that the elusive Frank
Lindenauer had been captured. It would be up to
Harris and the FBI to prove the case — that Lindenauer had impersonated a CIA agent to dupe John
and Louise Falconer into working for foreign ex-
tremists by convincing the couple that they were
helping their country in the war on terror.

"Then we turn ourselves in?" Meg whispered.

"Not yet," Aiden replied. "Not till we read in the
papers that Lindenauer admitted how he framed
Mom and Dad. That's when we go to the police."

He took a deep breath. "You know, we'll still be in trouble for this. Maybe serious trouble. We broke a lot of laws these past few weeks, and just being right about our parents might not get us off the hook. We'll probably wind up back in juvie."

Meg squared her jaw. "It's worth it," she said evenly. "Nothing was ever more worth it."

"I guess we'd better test the security gate," Aiden decided. "That's all we need — to have Hairless Frank right where we want him and the thing won't close." He reached up, took hold of the metal handle, and pulled. With a screech of unoiled parts, the iron barrier unrolled like a garage door and slammed against the concrete floor. The crash was earsplitting.

Hearts hammering, they surveyed the deserted gloom as the echoes died away. It was an awful lot of noise for two fugitives who were trying not to attract attention.

"If we can't trap him, maybe the noise will give him a heart attack," Meg offered with a nervous laugh.

"We'll trap him," Aiden said grimly. It was the confidence born of desperation. This would work because it *had* to. Otherwise, they would be leaving themselves completely defenseless against a professional assassin.

They ducked into the shadows around the side of Unit 130. Meg hugged her sweatshirt tight around her. It was still September, but Denver was high country, and the nights were growing colder.

At moments like this, she envied Aiden his infinite patience. She got fidgety waiting for two-minute microwave popcorn. This was no time to jump the gun.

And then a voice barked a single word: "*Freeze!*"

Shock . . . bewilderment . . . panic. Had Hairless Frank seen through their plan?

The Falconers wheeled, expecting to find themselves at the mercy of the assassin and his gun.

Instead, the man who stood twenty feet away was not much older than Aiden himself, with a round baby face. His chubby frame bulged inside his nylon windbreaker. An arm patch bore the logo of Rocky Mountain Security.

A night watchman! It wasn't Hairless Frank, but in his own way, this guy was just as bad. A security guard might hand them over to the police!

"Run — "

The cry was partway out of Meg's throat when a low growl reached her ears. At the end of a leash in the watchman's hand, a black-and-tan Doberman appeared, eyes glowing amber.

We can outrun the guard, she thought, *but never the dog.*

"What are you kids doing here?" the watchman demanded.

Meg spoke up. "Is this Jefferson Park?"

The words came quickly, almost by instinct. But surely this situation was too much even for her legendary ability to spin excuses. What could possibly explain their presence in a locked food terminal in the middle of the night?

"Jefferson Park?" The man stared at her. "It's one o'clock in the morning!"

"Jimmy got these night-vision goggles from his brother in the marines," Meg enthused. "We're all meeting in Jefferson Park to try them out."

"This isn't any park, kid. It's private property, and you're trespassing." The guard kept an iron grip on the leash, holding back the snarling Doberman.

"Really?" Meg's voice was pure innocent wonder. "Sorry, mister. We'll leave you alone — uh, how do you get out of here?"

For an instant, it seemed like the man was actually going to let them go. Then he looked at Aiden and his eyes narrowed. Meg could pass for a little kid, but Aiden was fifteen and tall for his age. He was a teenager, and to the security guard, teenagers meant trouble.

"You two are coming with me. We'll let the police decide what to do with you."

The Doberman bared its fangs.

 **7**

The administration building of the Denver Produce Terminal was a small flat structure not far from the Great West Supermarkets warehouse. It was the center of all business that didn't involve the loading and unloading of trucks.

It was also the base of operations of the night watchman. He reclined in a padded swivel chair, peering at a bank of mounted TV monitors. A control console enabled him to access dozens of cameras throughout the facility.

His prisoners tonight, Aiden and Meg, sat in utter misery in the locked room next door, waiting for the police officers who were on the way to arrest them.

"Maybe the cops won't realize it's us," Meg said hopefully. "What are we charged with — trespassing? Maybe they'll let us off with a warning."

"Oh, sure. Two kids with descriptions like ours, who refuse to give their parents' phone numbers? Come on, Meg — it'll take them about three seconds to figure out who we are." He shrugged help-lessly. "We should have made a break for it."

"Against a guard dog?" his sister challenged.

"At least then, we would have had a *chance*. You tamed a prehistoric pig — surely you could stare down one dog!"

"It showed me its teeth. That means it won't be stared down unless it's chewing on somebody. Look, we're caught. It stinks, but we're not going to change it with *woulda, shoulda, coulda*. How do we get out of here?"

Heart sinking, Aiden surveyed their surround-ings. There were only two ways out. The door — locked, with the watchman right behind it — and a small window with a security grate. Aiden tested the strength of the bars. They wouldn't budge. The floor was linoleum tile over concrete. The walls were solid. The ceiling —

He found himself staring up at a heating register above the window. "*Terror, Sweet Terror*," he mum-bled aloud.

"Huh?" And then Meg clued in. "You mean Dad's book?" In addition to his job as a professor of criminology, Dr. John Falconer was also the author of a series of detective thrillers.

"Don't you remember?" Aiden whispered. "Mac

Mulvey is locked inside the abandoned chocolate factory. The only escape is through — "

Meg followed his eyes to the register above them. "The heating ducts!" she finished breathlessly.

The Falconers pushed a chair under the vent. Aiden climbed onto the seat, reached over his head, and removed the grille. He peered up into the narrow aluminum tunnel that led to the guts of the building's ventilation system.

"Not exactly roomy in there," he commented.

"At least we know that tub-of-guts rent-a-cop won't be coming after us," Meg offered optimistically.

His sister held the chair steady while Aiden climbed onto the seat back and found a precarious balance. There were handholds on either side of the opening, and he was able to hoist himself up and in. The duct rose about eighteen inches before joining the main line. He could feel hot air blowing in his face as he squeezed his body around the tight corner.

The space was far too constricting for Aiden to turn around to check on Meg's progress. "Can you make it?" he asked.

In answer, a hand touched his ankle. "Right behind you, bro."

Aiden squinted into the silver-tinted darkness of the ductwork. It continued the full length of the building, branching off to deliver heat to the various rooms. He scrambled ahead in a clumsy motion that was somewhere between a crawl and a slither. Real crawling was impossible — the channel was too low and narrow.

To keep moving in such cramped space was back-breakingly difficult. His neck and spine ached, and he was drenched in sweat.

Meg, too, was aware of the discomfort. "If Dad ever *tried* this stuff instead of just writing about it," she panted, "he wouldn't be so quick to put Mac Mulvey through such torture."

All at once, Aiden drew in a sharp breath. Directly in front of him, a heating line dropped to the next room. Through the mesh of the grille he could see the pudgy security guard six feet below.

He twisted around to signal Meg to be silent, but his elbow smacked into the wall of the ductwork. The metal reverberated like the banging of a gong.

He held his breath, eyes glued to the husky form beneath him. The guard did not react.

They wriggled on, struggling for every millimeter of progress. Aiden had never before suffered from claustrophobia, but now he felt the aluminum squeezing him on all sides, crushing him —

Keep it together! he ordered himself, battling his own mind as much as the closeness of the tunnel.

The supply grille leading to the next room beckoned from below.

No — not far enough away.

He dragged himself past the opening, and past the next one, too. He was afraid he might black out when at long last the metallic floor fell away to the register in the ceiling of the last room on this side of the building.

Sudden terror — how was he going to swing his legs into the opening? Pressed in on all sides, he strained to maneuver, but could not contort himself into the right shape. In desperation, he crawled straight down into the shaft. Upended in the tube, he hung on with his sneakers against the sweat-slick aluminum.

Suddenly, the rubber soles lost their grip on the metal, and he was falling. He struck the grille head-first, knocking it open on its hinge. Cringing, he braced himself for a devastating fall. There was nothing between his cranium and the hard floor eight feet away.

A hand gripped tight onto his left ankle.

"Gotcha!" came Meg's strained voice. And then, "Whoa!"

His weight dragged her through the opening, and they were both dropping. At the last second, Aiden got his arms wrapped around his head for protection. He hit the floor and barrel-rolled onto his back. The impact knocked the wind out of him.

A split second later, Meg landed right on top of him. Any breath he had managed to recover was gone again. Both lay there, stunned.

Meg was the first to recover. "You okay?"

Aiden sat up. "Let's get out of here!" His eyes traveled to the window. It had the same security grill as their detention room, but this one was ajar.

They eased the sash up, climbed out over the sill, and dropped to the ground. A few seconds later, they were scampering off, swallowed up by the night.

Aiden tugged on Meg's arm, slowing her down. "Wait —"

"Move it, bro!"

"We can't leave yet," he insisted. "Hairless Frank is coming."

"So are the cops!"

"We don't know if we'll ever get another shot at the guy, Meg. If we could trap him tonight, being arrested would be worth it. At least the police would be there to bust him along with us."

Her heart swelled with hope, but she was still torn. "You'd better be right about this," she muttered as they made their way through the shadows in the direction of Unit 129.

Aiden wasn't sure about anything. He only knew that this might be their one chance to end the long nightmare. Passing it up was unthinkable, no matter what the risk.

They approached Unit 129 cautiously. With no watch, they could only guess at the time. Hairless Frank might already be in there, lying in wait. Aiden reached into his pocket and fingered the heavy padlock he'd brought from the farm. It was such a simple process that lay ahead of them: Roll down the gate, slap on the lock, and the deed would be done.

But with everything on the line, with the real Frank Lindenauer in there, Aiden wondered if his hands would be shaking too wildly to perform the simple operation of snapping the metal staple into place.

With a sudden start, Meg took her brother's arm and grasped it hard enough to splinter bone.

"What?" he whispered.

In answer, she moved so close that he could see her face, inches away, in the near-zero light. He felt her breath as she mouthed the words: "He's here."

8

"Where?"

The hiss had barely left Aiden's lips when he heard it. A footfall, then another — not inside Unit 129, but on the gravel walkway — right beside them. Whatever courage came from the feeling of the lock in his hand evaporated in a heartbeat.

There was a rasping sound, and a match flared, illuminating three faces — his own, his sister's, and —

"Who are *you*?" Meg demanded.

The man before them was middle-aged, with a few days' growth of beard, long stringy hair, and unmatched rumpled clothing. He might have been a homeless person. He was *not* Frank Lindenauer.

He looked at them in surprise. "You're just a couple of kids!"

"What are you doing here?" Aiden demanded. "What do you want from us?"

"Don't you recognize your Uncle Frank?"

Meg was in a state of high agitation. "Get away from us, you — "

The match burned down, and he dropped it and lit another. When the glow returned, he had backed away a couple of steps. "Hey, don't get upset. I'm harmless. I go through the personal ads — sometimes I can make a few bucks pretending to be somebody I'm not. I didn't realize you were kids."

Aiden felt the air go out of him like a collapsing balloon. The realization overwhelmed his relief at being in no danger from this newcomer, and even from their breakout from the administration building.

It was a hoax. They had *never* reached Frank Lindenauer.

Justice for Mom and Dad was as far away as it had ever been.

Apologizing all the way, the impostor scrambled off into the night, leaving Aiden and Meg hanging on to each other for mutual comfort. They had faced too many reversals of fortune in too short a time: capture, escape, followed by coming face-to-face with the ultimate enemy — only to find out it wasn't him.

"We should get out of here, bro," Meg said finally. "We don't want to wait around for the cops."

"It was a scam, Meg," Aiden mourned, his voice hollow. "Frank Lindenauer didn't get in touch with us. What if he never does?"

"We've got to get ourselves home if we're going to have a chance to find that out," she reminded him wearily.

Staying in the shadows, they skirted the fence until they found the opening they'd used to get in. Minutes after that, they were in the truck, starting for the Turnbull farm.

They had barely rounded the first corner when a squad car appeared, heading in the other direction. They held their collective breath and prayed as it passed them. In the rearview mirror, Aiden watched it pull up to the food terminal gate.

"No siren, no hurry," he commented. "I guess they don't know it's us."

It was about time something went right.

Five-thirty A.M. If it hadn't been for his kid sister, Aiden's depression would have been total. At least he had Meg to milk the cows for him. Cleaning up their stalls, however, was still his responsibility. So he shoveled, eyes watering from the stench, while she milked away.

For once, he was almost grateful for the manure smell. The Falconers were operating on less than three hours of sleep. The reek was the only thing keeping them both awake.

Shortly after sunrise, the shooting started.

Meg shuddered on her milking stool. "Man, I am *never* going to get used to that. If Mr. Turnbull doesn't finish the porch soon, his nail gun is going to give me heart failure."

Aiden had to agree. Every cracking discharge was a reminder of the many gunshots Hairless Frank had aimed in their direction. How many more lay in their future?

And, more important, will we even find him again?

The endless barn chores ran one into the other, until Aiden was practically asleep on his feet.

"Hey!" Meg said suddenly, pouring the last pailful of milk into the larger canister. "Hear that?"

Aiden paused to listen. "What?"

"Nothing. The shooting's stopped."

In his exhausted state, it took Aiden precious seconds to process what this might mean. By the time he glanced out the barn door, Zephraim Turnbull's right crutch was already thumping through it.

It was too late to call out a warning, but none was necessary. The fugitives were so attuned to each other's thoughts and emotions that messages seemed to flash between them by radar. A glance at Aiden's face was all Meg needed to get the one-word message: *Disappear!*

She dove headfirst behind a stack of hay bales, covering herself with loose straw from the floor of the stall.

"Good morning, Mr. Turnbull!" Aiden exclaimed, much too heartily.

The farmer swung his way into the middle of the barn and looked around. "Place is clean, milking done," he observed grudgingly. "I would have bet money you didn't know one end of a cow from the other. Only hired you 'cause I needed a warm body to seem like he's working my farm. But you're not as hopeless as you look."

"Thanks," said Aiden, not really sure the faint praise had been a compliment. He didn't mention that it was taking two of them to achieve such non-hopelessness. "Uh — how are you enjoying the computer?"

"Fool thing!" the farmer spat. "Some voice inside keeps saying I've got mail. But I can't for the life of me figure out how to get at it!"

A roaring came up in Aiden's ears, and he fought to stay calm. Was that e-mail message for the farmer, or could it be for falx@zipnet.usa? And if so, was it the message they'd been waiting for?

"I'll come over later," he promised, keeping his voice steady, "and we'll see what you've got."

Turnbull acknowledged this with a grunt. "One more thing," he added, looking uncomfortable. "Do you happen to have a girl living here with you?"

The question came from so far out in left field that Aiden was turned to stone. The result was an expression so shocked and so bewildered that Turnbull took it for innocence.

"I didn't think so. Sorry for even asking. It's that vulture Holyfield. If he'd spend half as much time minding his own business as he does minding mine, he'd be so rich that he wouldn't need my farm to sell to Mountain View Homes!"

Aiden's head was spinning. This wasn't a conversation he wanted to continue, especially with his sister hiding behind a bale of hay twenty feet away. "I don't understand," he managed. "Mr. Holyfield told you this? He doesn't know me!"

"His spies hang around here like cheap curtains. Sorry to put you on the spot, Gary. But when he told me about you and this girl, I had to get to the bottom of it. He just wants me to fire you so I'll have no hired man." He began thump-swinging for the barn door. "Anyway, my problem, not yours."

Meg didn't come out of hiding until she heard the sharp reports of the nail gun resume. Then she emerged, pale and shaken.

"Wow!" she breathed. "I was sure all that Holyfield business was just in Mr. Turnbull's head!"

Aiden nodded. "This farm really *is* being watched. We've got to be more careful."

Meg looked thoughtful. "At least Mr. Turnbull didn't believe him — about seeing me, I mean."

Aiden was the worrier of the pair. "It doesn't matter whether Turnbull believes him or not. Somebody got a look at you. And I'm in plain sight.

Sooner or later, someone is going to put two and two together and come up with Falconer. Remember, the FBI's offering twenty-five thousand bucks for us."

"The clock's ticking," she agreed sadly. "What are the chances this new mail has something to do with us?"

"It probably does," he said dejectedly. "But how do we know it won't turn out to be another small-time crook like last night?"

Yet hours later, when Aiden looked at the message, he knew instantly that it was no hoax. The name Frank Lindenauer appeared nowhere in it, nor was there any proof that the assassin was its source. Its style spoke for itself — brief, cold, all business.

It read simply:

When and where?

"I don't like it," Meg commented as Aiden parked the truck in the very same grove of trees outside the Denver Produce Terminal. "Two days ago, we almost got caught here. Couldn't we have found somewhere else for this?"

"No time," her brother replied grimly. "We can't run around Denver, scouting out deserted places that lock from the outside. It's here or it's nowhere."

"But what if that night watchman — "

"He heard the noise when we tested the security gate," he cut her off impatiently. "We don't have to do that tonight. Come on, Meg. We can't go around changing the plan every five minutes. This isn't a game!"

"Okay, okay, don't get so touchy. We're on the same side, remember?"

As they made their way to the fence, Meg regarded her brother uneasily. What was up with Aiden these last few days? For weeks, he had held it together under the most desperate of circumstances, when their chances of helping their parents had seemed like a trillion to one. Yet now, with capturing Hairless Frank actually within reach, he was freaking out.

It's almost as if he's afraid of the opportunity to finally get it done. He's petrified that he'll blow the marathon in the home stretch.

Being *close* was bothering Aiden. Instead of celebrating it, he was letting it drive him crazy.

They slipped under the fence and made their way over to the abandoned section, giving the administration building a wide berth.

Fatso and his mutt aren't invited to this party. There was only one name on the guest list — Frank Lindenauer.

The moon provided no more than a dim glow behind cloud cover, so the area around Unit 129 was completely unlit. They paused about fifty feet away, gazing into the blackness of the garage-sized storage locker. It looked empty, but —

"What if he came early, and he's in there waiting for us?" Meg whispered.

Aiden picked up a rock the size of a baseball and hurled it. It struck the gravel a few feet in front of the opening and skittered inside the unit, skipping across the concrete floor.

They ducked. If Hairless Frank was in there, the response would probably come in a hail of gunfire. But there was no sound from the storage locker, and none from the surrounding area, either.

They had beaten him here. The trap was baited.

They hid themselves in the blackness of the unit directly across from 129 and waited for their quarry to arrive.

In their nervousness, they had left themselves more than an hour to wait. The tension of those sixty minutes was as tight as the cable of a suspension bridge. Time slowed to a near standstill. In the suffocating silence, Meg found herself concentrating on the sound of distant trucks gearing up and down on some unseen interstate. It was the perfect symbol for what it had come to mean to be a Falconer. Somewhere out there, life went on as normal for everybody else.

But here we are, trapped in amber, waiting for the next flame-up, wondering if this will be the one that incinerates us.

The childish phrase almost came to her lips: *It isn't fair.* Yet this nightmare had gone so far beyond fair that the word had ceased to have meaning. There was no fair, and there hadn't been for more than a year. Not since the FBI battering ram had reduced their front door to toothpicks.

Lost in sad thoughts, she almost missed the moment when it came. Only the stiffening of her brother's lean frame alerted her. She saw the flashlight first, then the shadowy figure carrying it. The diffused beam caused the man to appear in silhouette — the bald head, bull neck, stocky, powerful build. It was him, no question about it.

Hairless Frank.

Meg felt an arctic blast of pure fright. Yet, in a strangely detached way, she couldn't help thinking of that moment in every shark movie when the great white makes its first leisurely pass, lethal and unhurried. Their predator was every bit as deadly. He moved at a measured pace, confident, and sure of the ultimate kill.

He didn't walk straight into Unit 129. To their dismay, he began to pace the area around it, shining his flashlight in doorways and down alleyways. They crouched, frozen with fear as the beam played ever closer to their hiding spot, even lighting up the empty locker behind them.

Meg bit her lip to keep from screaming. In another few seconds, they would be discovered. What then? Fight? Run?

Miraculously, the circle of light skipped them. Meg allowed herself to start breathing again. Eventually, the shadowy figure was satisfied that he was alone. The blinding torch turned away from them, and Hairless Frank stepped inside Unit 129.

The rat had entered the trap.

11

The Falconers watched, tensing for action, waiting for the right moment. Hairless Frank moved farther back in the storage locker, sweeping the interior with his flashlight beam. Four steps — five steps — then six.

Aiden breathed a single word. "Now."

Like phantom figures, the Falconers bounded across the lane, their feet barely touching the ground, their approach soundless. Aiden reached up, grabbed the gate, and began hauling it down in a screech of metal. Meg added her strength, and they rolled the heavy barrier until it crashed against the cement floor.

The howl of outrage that came from Unit 129 was barely human. A huge impact rocked the gate from inside.

Meg pressed down on the handholds with all her might. "The lock, Aiden! *The lock!*"

His fingers fluttering with panic, Aiden fumbled

the padlock and very nearly dropped it. Eyes bulging with equal parts concentration and terror, he rattled the staple through the double ring of the gate and slammed the lock shut.

Hairless Frank hit the metal again, then grabbed hold and tried to lift it. It wouldn't budge.

"I'm going to kill you!" he roared. "Just like I should have killed your parents before the feds got them!"

"You *did* kill them!" The words poured out of Meg, bubbling up by the force of her emotion. "You killed our whole family when you framed them!"

Aiden pulled her back from the door and held her tightly. "It's over, Meg! We got him!"

Was it possible? Could the endless nightmare actually be coming to an end?

"Harris!" she gasped. "We have to call Harris and the FBI!"

The response came in the form of a gunshot. The bullet tore a hole in the gate and sang past Meg's ear.

Aiden threw her to the ground and covered her body with his own. More shots followed, ricocheting all around them.

"We've got to get away from here!" Aiden rasped. "He's trying to kill us from inside!"

Meg peered past her brother's shoulders at the

gated Unit 129. An orderly line of bullet holes marched down the side of the corrugated metal. As she watched, another shot burst through, taking off a corner of the padlock.

It came to her in a rush of horror. "Aiden — he's not shooting at us! He's shooting at the lock!"

Another blast — this one ripping into the actual mechanism of the padlock. Small parts scattered, raining down on the gravel. The Falconers stared in disbelief. The lock was disintegrating before their very eyes.

Unbelievable! Meg thought in rising hysteria. *We've got him in a concrete bunker, behind a steel door, and we're still not safe!*

The next shot struck the lock dead center, sending a shower of metal fragments spraying in all directions. Unbelievably, the staple was still threaded through the rings. But most of the body was gone. It would not survive another bullet.

Hairless Frank would soon be free.

Meg looked around wildly, as if she actually expected to find a weapon powerful enough to stand up to this assassin and his gun.

It took Aiden to haul her to her feet. *"Run!"*

She was too flustered to think straight. "But he'll get away!"

"How are we supposed to stop him?"

The depth of their peril was rammed home with the last pistol discharge. They heard the lock drop to the ground, but they weren't around to see it.

They flew, pounding through the food terminal with no thought for being quiet or avoiding the night watchman and his dog. It was flight at its most primitive and basic. They heard the screech and crash of the metal gate being torn open.

The beast was loose.

Meg tried to estimate their head start. Fifty feet? A hundred?

Not enough, she thought grimly. The first shot was just a crack. But the second came closer, whining past her ear like a rocket-powered mosquito.

They sprinted for the fence, dropping to the ground and rolling through the gap. They gained a little time when their pursuer wouldn't fit through the opening and had to clamber over the top. But if Hairless Frank lagged behind, his weapon made up the difference.

Nobody can outrun bullets.

In a hail of gunfire, they barreled across the road to the thicket where their pickup was parked. Keys already in hand, Aiden raced for the cab. But Meg, whose legs were shorter, was lagging behind. With

Hairless Frank gaining on her, she took the fastest route to cover. She vaulted over the tailgate and landed in the flatbed amid bushel baskets of turnips.

There was a crack, and a bullet slammed into the basket in front of her. She shut her eyes and waited for the impact that would mean she'd been hit. It never came.

Unbelievable! A turnip is dense enough to stop bullets!

A horrible thought struck her — Aiden! He was at the wheel, totally exposed. She peered over the top of the basket and saw Hairless Frank, gun arm raised, taking careful aim at her brother in the cab.

The turnip materialized in her hand before she realized what she had in mind. She flung it without aiming — there was no time. Yet the aim was true. The spiraling vegetable struck their attacker on the side of the head, sending him staggering backward.

The truck's engine roared to life.

Her voice bordered on dementia. "Go! Go! *Go!*"

The vehicle blasted forward, battering her with spilled turnips. Meg didn't mind the rough ride. She was grateful to be out of there.

12

Farmer Turnbull's grocery lists were short and always the same: canned goods, Ovaltine, English muffins, and peanut butter, extra-crunchy. Since Aiden had signed on as hired hand two weeks before, the farmer had already gone through four jars of the stuff. Aiden could only assume it was his breakfast, lunch, and dinner.

He was coming out of the supermarket with the usual provisions when a uniformed sheriff's deputy stepped in front of him, blocking his path. "I think you'd better come with me."

Aiden was completely flummoxed. In the past weeks, he had eluded hundreds of police officers, government agents, and juvenile corrections officials. He had beaten mass manhunts and wiggled out of tight spots that would have overwhelmed Houdini. Yet here, carrying Zephraim Turnbull's peanut butter in Aberdeen, Colorado, this sad excuse for a town, both mind and body shut down.

One of the most notorious fugitives in America made no attempt to flee, or even resist. He allowed himself and his grocery bag to be loaded into the backseat of a squad car without lifting a finger in his own defense.

It was during the short drive to the sheriff's office that he finally offered a feeble protest. "What's this about? I have to pick up Mr. Turnbull from his doctor's appointment."

The deputy grimaced. "I'll phone over there and let them know you're not coming."

The sheriff's office was located in a tiny strip mall that also hosted a dry cleaner and a veterinary clinic. It was a strange place, Aiden decided, for the quest to save the Falconer family to come to an end. Of course, Meg would try to fight on by herself. His gallant little sister would never give up. But she had no chance alone. Aiden was the one who could pass for older, who could get a job or drive a car. Meg wouldn't even have an answer to the question, *Why aren't you in school?*

God, what was he going to do about her? Rat her out? Never! Yet how could he leave her all alone, hiding on the Turnbull farm, wondering what had happened to her brother?

Our quest is dead.

But had it ever really been alive? Last night's showdown in the produce terminal had answered that question. The road to clearing their parents had always gone through Frank Lindenauer. And Frank Lindenauer had always been unbeatable.

The deputy ushered him inside and sat him down by a desk. Aiden braced himself for the worst: *You're Aiden Falconer, wanted in fifty states and the District of Columbia. You have the right to remain silent . . .*

Instead, the man said, "Name?"

"Graham. Gary Graham." Was this some kind of trap?

"I'll need to see your driver's license, or some other form of identification."

"I — I left my wallet back at the farm."

"How'd you pay for those groceries, then?"

"Mr. Turnbull has an account with the store." Aiden was beginning to take heart. Was it possible that the guy had no idea who he had arrested? And if not, what did they want with him?

"Listen," he ventured, "Mr. Turnbull has a broken leg. He needs me. Please tell me what's going on."

In answer, the deputy reached into a drawer, pulled out a huge turnip, and slapped it onto the desk blotter between them. Lodged in the depth of the turnip's solid flesh was a nine-millimeter bullet.

"How do you explain this?" the officer demanded.

"I didn't shoot that thing!" Aiden defended himself. "Who shoots a turnip? I don't even own a gun."

Why were these small-town cops searching a local truck farmer's basket of vegetables? They couldn't know about the encounter with Hairless Frank last night — could they?

The man sneered in his face. "And I suppose you can't explain the bullet hole in the tailgate of your truck, either?"

"That's right, I can't!" Aiden exclaimed. "Because I know nothing about it!" He wasn't sure just how outraged he should act. His confidence was back because, apparently, he hadn't been identified as one of the fugitive Falconers. He had to use that to bluster his way out of here. Sooner or later, it would dawn on this officer that he had every right to arrest Aiden for driving without a license.

Then they'll take my fingerprints. And when they run them through the computer . . .

He couldn't let that happen, but he was unsure of what to say. Meg was the expert when it came to situations like this.

The office door opened, and there stood Zephraim Turnbull, his weathered face a thundercloud. He planted his crutches and swung himself into the room, landing with a plop beside Aiden.

Aiden jumped up to give the farmer his chair, but Turnbull barked, "I don't need to sit! We're not staying!"

The deputy looked uneasy. "Zeph, stay out of this. This is a police investigation. It's for your protection."

Turnbull laughed mirthlessly. "You think I need protection from *him*? How long have you known me?"

The deputy held up the turnip so the farmer could see the bullet hole. "See this? There's a hole just like it in the tailgate of your truck."

"And you think *Gary* put it there?" Turnbull was outraged. "That'd be a neat trick — driving and shooting out your own tailgate at the same time!"

"Look, people are worried about you, Zeph," the man tried to explain. "We had a call from a concerned citizen —"

"Who just happened to be snooping in my truck?" the farmer exploded. "It's Holyfield, right? He brought you this vegetable to make trouble for me!"

The deputy was tight-lipped. "I'm not at liberty to discuss — "

"I knew it! He's been harassing me for months and here's the proof. He sent one of his goons into my vehicle to steal this turnip!"

"It still doesn't explain the bullet."

"Oh, that's rich." Turnbull's voice dripped with sarcasm. "My hired man can shoot a turnip, but not Holyfield. I've already told you about his private investigators trespassing on my property, interfering with my livestock!"

"I've been meaning to talk to you about that, Zeph. There's another complaint — about a vicious pig."

"You know what's happening here!" Turnbull accused. "They want to get rid of Gary because they know I can't work the farm and they can break my lease! What kind of police protection are you providing when my landlord can shoot up my truck just to intimidate me? Why aren't you questioning Holyfield instead of my hired hand?" He picked his grocery bag up off the desk and handed it to Aiden. "Come on, Gary. We're going home."

And they left the police station, Aiden holding the door for the old man thumping along on his crutches.

"Sorry about this, Mr. Turnbull," Aiden mumbled once they were outside.

His employer looked at him sharply. "What have you got to be sorry about? I should be apologizing to you. Didn't mean to get you mixed up in this brouhaha between Holyfield and me."

"That's okay," Aiden assured him, eyes averted. He felt a twinge of guilt over the fact that he was forced to mislead the farmer. A plan was beginning to take shape in his mind. One way or another, he knew he would not be Mr. Turnbull's hired man for very much longer.

The hired hand's apartment was an extension of the barn — a neat studio with a living room/bedroom combination, a tiny kitchen, and an even tinier bathroom. The walls would have closed in on anybody. But Meg was going stir-crazy.

Ever since they'd heard that Holyfield's people had spotted a girl around the farm, the rules had changed for Meg. She couldn't risk being seen again. Mr. Turnbull had dismissed the first accusation. But if the landlord came up with real proof, like a photograph, the farmer would have to take notice. So except for milking times, she didn't dare set foot out the door. The blinds were drawn, so she never felt the sun. It was like she was back at Sunnydale Farm, the juvenile prison. Worse — she couldn't even risk flushing the toilet if Aiden wasn't at home.

Where *was* Aiden? His days were busy, but he usually popped in just often enough to keep her from melting down through sheer boredom. She knew he'd had to drive the farmer into town for a doctor's appointment, but they were definitely back. She could tell by the relentless *blam-blam-blam* of Turnbull working on his porch. The nail gun sounded just like Hairless Frank using them for target practice. It was enough to give her a nervous breakdown.

She checked the clock on the stove. Soon it would be time to bring in the cows for the late-afternoon milking. Aiden had to do that. Plus he was the one who made sure the coast was clear so she could come out into the barn.

Come on, bro. Where are you?

He finally turned up around four-thirty with a small parcel and a grim expression.

"Radio Shack?" Meg read the label. "I hope it's a Game Boy. I've been losing my mind in this place!"

He opened the bag and took out a tiny metal box about the size of a credit card.

Meg stared. "What's that?"

"A voice-activated tape recorder," her brother informed her. "Listen — last night proved one thing. We are *never* going to capture Frank Lindenauer. The only way to catch him is to kill him, and we can't do that because he's the person who can prove Mom and Dad are innocent."

She stuck out her jaw. "You sound like you're giving up. There's no giving up in this."

"Right," he agreed. "But we have to try something different."

"Like what?"

"Like getting him to confess on tape how he framed Mom and Dad."

She was growing exasperated. "Why would he do that?"

"He won't know that he's being recorded," her brother explained patiently. "We'll set up another meeting, and I'll wear this under my shirt. I'll talk to him, get him to admit what he did. And he will — because he thinks he's going to kill me."

Meg was alarmed. "He *is* going to kill you!"

Aiden nodded reluctantly. "Maybe. But even if I'm dead, you'll still have the tape to take to the FBI."

In eleven years of sometimes stormy relations, Meg could not remember being so angry with her brother. Words welled up inside her — screaming words that would have drowned out the nail gun. But she had to be quiet. So she pounded on his shoulders with balled-up fists and hissed out her rage.

"Who do you think you are? There are no suicide

missions in this family! What would Mom and Dad say if they knew you were trying to buy their freedom with your life?"

"They won't say anything," Aiden replied tersely, "because I'm not asking them. Listen to what happened to me today." He told her about the near miss with the deputy sheriff.

"So what?" she snapped. "We've had closer calls than that!"

"You think so?" Aiden retorted. "We're talking about a cop who knows where to find me, who might show up anytime and ask to see my driver's license. And don't forget that Holyfield guy, who has a real interest in making trouble for Mr. Turnbull. He knows about you. Do you think he's going to let that lie? He'll keep snooping and snooping until he finds out something we don't want him to know. Our days here are numbered, Meg."

"Then we'll move on!" she pleaded. "We've done it a dozen times! We'll start over! It isn't fun, but it's more fun than being dead!"

"We're too famous to be out there," Aiden said flatly. "You think everybody's like Mr. Turnbull, who never reads the paper or turns on the TV? We'll be captured, and soon. And even if we stay free, what if Hairless Frank disappears again? It's a miracle we found him the first time. No more running. This is where we make our stand!"

"He'll kill you!" she repeated tearfully. "And there's no guarantee that you'll get the evidence we need!"

"Remember what he said when we had him locked up?" Aiden reminded her. "'I'm going to kill you like I should have killed your parents before the feds got them.' He's a talker. In the Mac Mulvey books the bad guy always spills his guts because he doesn't think it can hurt him."

Meg thought her head would explode from the effort of holding back a shriek of frustration. "You don't bet your life on Mac Mulvey!"

"I'm betting on Dad," Aiden said stubbornly. "The criminal mind is his life's work — Mom's, too. People like Hairless Frank can't resist bragging when they think they've won. I *know* I can get him to admit he framed our parents!"

Meg felt a new depth of despair. *I should have seen it coming. He's been winding himself tighter and tighter every day. I should have known something awful was going to happen.*

Aloud, she said, "I can't let you do it, Aiden. You're not thinking straight."

"My thinking is fine. It's time for all this to be over. One way or another, it has to end."

"That's where you're wrong," she told him. "I'd rather it went on forever than have you dead. I'd rather be in jail *with* you than free without you. Don't leave me — *please*!"

He hugged her, but all he would say was, "I'll get the cows." And out he went, leaving her trembling and emotionally exhausted.

He was going to do it! He was actually going to do this insane thing! Her wimpy brother, who once dialed 9-1-1 because he saw a bat in their attic, was about to embark on a kamikaze mission. From his manner, she just knew that there was nothing she could do to stop him.

After the evening milking, when Meg was back inside her prison for the night, Aiden went to the residence to "help" Mr. Turnbull with his computer. She knew exactly what that meant. Aiden was e-mailing Hairless Frank to reestablish contact. He was putting his plan into action.

It's like watching a car slide off an icy road. You can see it happening, even predict its course, but you can't change the final result.

When he returned, she asked, "Did you send it?"

"Yes."

"Any answer?"

"Not yet."

But there would be an answer, she knew. And it would come soon. Hairless Frank would not pass up the opportunity for an easy kill.

Later that night, she tossed and turned on the sitting room couch, tormented by terrifying pictures: her brother, dead; her parents, devastated; herself, alone. A few feet away, Aiden slept like a baby in the single bed, serene and undisturbed. Aiden, the most fidgety sleeper in the world, sawing logs like he hadn't a care.

He's made up his mind.

The die was cast. This was definitely going to happen. No force in the universe could change it.

She took a deep cleansing breath. *Well, if I can't stop him, at least I can do everything in my power to make sure Frank Lindenauer doesn't kill him.*

And there was only one way to accomplish that.

14

The crowing of the rooster woke Aiden at exactly 4:51 A.M. God, he hated that lousy bird! What idiot said roosters crow at sunup? This thing went off like an alarm clock when the sun was still two time zones away. Leave it to Mr. Turnbull to have an East Coast rooster disturbing people on Colorado time!

It drove him crazy that Meg always slept through it. The fact that little aggravations never seemed to touch Meg was, in itself, a little aggravation for her brother.

"Pssst," he whispered. "You awake?"

No answer.

"Meg?"

He knew instantly that something was wrong. The tone of the room was off. He felt — alone. He jumped out of bed and went over to the couch. No Meg. The blanket she used was neatly folded. On top of it lay a piece of paper, which read:

*I know you're going to be mad at me, but I
can't let you throw your life away. One day
you'll see this is the best thing.*

Love,

Meg

*P.S. If I ever had to go on the run again, I'd
pick you to run with me.*

He read and reread the note, the blood pounding
in his ears. She was gone! *Gone!* Worse, she'd run
out on him just when things were coming to a head.
If she had been standing there, he would have
cheerfully strangled her.

How could she do this to him? How? After all
they'd been through together — the near misses, the
narrow escapes, the rescues! Both he and Meg had
risked their lives for each other at least a dozen
times! He had run through smoke and flame to bust
her out of a burning building! She had allowed herself to be hit by a pickup truck just for a ride to the
hospital where she knew he was being held! How
could she walk away from that kind of loyalty?
How could she walk away from *him*? How could
she walk away from Mom and Dad and their one
chance to save the family?

He stood there in the middle of the room, chest

heaving with anger and hurt. He knew exactly what she was up to. She thought he couldn't pull this off without her, that he didn't have the guts to go through with it alone!

Well, she was seriously wrong about that!

Not that he relished the idea of taking on Hairless Frank solo. But Meg wouldn't be directly involved in that anyway. Her part was to stay hidden from the killer, and then make sure the assassin's taped confession was delivered to the FBI. After all, there was a pretty good chance that Aiden himself would not be in any condition to make that delivery.

I might be dead.

A wave of dread rolled over him, washed out by an undertow of self-pity. These could be his final days — his final hours, even. How could she leave him to spend them alone?

Oh, grow up! he told himself. *These are the cards you've been dealt; this is the hand you play.*

It would work without Meg. Even if the worst happened and he did not survive, the police would find the recorder on his body and play the confession that would clear his parents. It wouldn't be easy for Mom and Dad to lose their son, but at least they'd be free.

He reread his sister's note, and almost choked on

the P.S. How could she do this? On top of everything else he had to contend with, now he had to
worry about an eleven-year-old girl, out there alone
in the big bad world.

Aw, come on, Meg! Where are you?

The bus rolled into Denver's central terminal at
seven-thirty A.M. Out stepped a few day-trippers, a
dozen commuters, and a young girl with her dark
hair cut so short that she could easily have passed for
a boy.

Although it was early, she had been on the go for
a very long time. She had stolen out of the hired
hand's apartment at four in the morning, taking
with her nothing but the clothes on her back and a
little money. Her escape had gone unnoticed by
everyone except Bernard. So it was that a three-
hundred-pound attack pig had received the farewell
hug she hadn't dared give her brother.

"Go easy on Aiden," she'd whispered, stroking
the creature's massive flank. "He's a good guy —
even if he's gone completely nuts."

Next had come a four-mile walk to town along
deserted roads, through suffocating darkness. Sunrise and the arrival of the bus had improved her

mood a little. But the burden of what she was about to do still hung heavy on her heart.

During this whole nightmare, stretching back to Mom and Dad's arrest, through foster homes, juvenile detention, and these weeks on the run — in all that time, the lone bright spot had been the fact that Aiden and Meg had managed to stay together. True, they had gotten separated a few times. But in those cases, they had fought tooth and nail to be reunited.

Now here she was, running away from him — on purpose. Every single cell in her body screamed out against what she was doing. How could she betray her brother?

I'm not betraying him. I'm trying to save his life.

Well, at least she knew exactly where she was going. She found a bank of pay phones and looked up the address she wanted. The fact that she was planning to go there was enough to make her laugh and cry at the same time. It was the last place on Earth she'd ever expected to visit of her own free will.

A short taxi ride later, she found herself standing in front of the Denver office of the Federal Bureau of Investigation.

She stared at the doors as if they were ringed with jagged teeth. Her fugitive instincts were sharp. Police were to be avoided at all costs. FBI headquarters would be like walking into the belly of the beast.

She stopped halfway up the walkway and looked around, searching for a reason not to go inside.

Don't be a baby. You're doing the right thing.

And then she spotted the Starbucks across the street. A parade of images marched through her mind, all of them six feet seven inches tall. Agent Emmanuel Harris. Every time she had seen the hated J. Edgar Giraffe, he had been toting an extra-large cup of coffee. Even on CNN, the man who had arrested John and Louise Falconer always seemed to have the Starbucks logo on a hot cup in his meaty hand.

Through the tinted windows of the coffee shop, she could see a number of patrons seated at café tables. One of them was a foot taller in the saddle than all the others.

Taking a deep breath for courage, she crossed the street and paused in front of the door.

For Aiden, she reminded herself, and entered.

There he was, not ten feet away, the destroyer of the Falconer family.

He looked up and took in the sight of one of the young fugitives he had been tracking for seven thousand miles. The shock tightened his grip on the hot cup, and a geyser of coffee shot straight up through the spout, splattering the ceiling.

He leaped to his feet and put an iron grip on her wrist.

"It's okay," she said. "I'm not going anywhere."

"Where's your brother?" he demanded.

"He's safe," she replied. "For now."

"What does that mean? Is he safe or isn't he?"

All at once, the tension pressed down on her, turning her legs to jelly. Abruptly, she collapsed into the chair opposite the big FBI man.

"We need to talk."

15

"How can I help Aiden if you won't tell me where he is?"

Agent Harris was nearly purple in the face. The interrogation of Margaret Falconer had been going on all morning and into the afternoon. And like all his dealings with the two young fugitives, it was fruitless, and frustrating to the point of pain.

She reclined on a swivel chair in his tiny office, her arms folded resolutely in front of her. "You expect me to rat on my own brother?"

"Yes!" he exploded. Because of the close quarters, he was interviewing her from halfway out into the hall. "You're here, aren't you? You gave yourself up to protect him. But I can't keep him safe if I can't get to him!"

She stuck out her jaw. "The minute I tell you where he is, you'll arrest him."

"That's what protect *means*," the agent insisted.

"We have to bring him in so your hairless friend can't get at him. Listen, Margaret — "

"It's Meg."

"All right — Meg. Aiden's in more danger than you know. That bald assassin who's after you — I have reason to believe he's the man you call Frank Lindenauer!"

"Duh," she taunted. "We figured that out already. Now tell me something I *don't* know." She looked around scornfully. "Nice office, by the way. The size of a closet. Oh, excuse me, it *is* a closet."

Harris regarded her warily. It was obvious Meg's arrogant toughness was an act. Under her bravado, she was terrified. And why not, after all she'd been through? But the game had clearly changed. These past weeks, the Falconer kids had moved mountains to avoid capture, in an unlikely mix of desperation and daring brilliance. For this girl to turn herself in *now* meant that something big must have happened.

What that might be, Agent Harris could only guess. But his instincts told him it had something to do with the reason Meg suddenly believed her brother needed protection.

The agent took a deep breath. "All right — you

don't have to tell me where he is. Give me a hint. Is he lost? Hurt? Sick?"

"Yeah," Meg snorted. "Sick in the head would be more like it."

Harris pounced on the clue. "He's going to try something crazy — and you can't stop him on your own?"

He could actually see the girl tuning him out, her eyes glazing over as she retreated inside herself. She had come here ready to cooperate in order to save her brother — Harris was certain of that. But in the presence of the agent who had upended her world, she had shut down.

Harris almost understood. He was the one who had sent John and Louise Falconer to prison for life. Of course, she blamed him for everything that had happened to her family. The truth was, Harris blamed himself. Every day he was becoming more convinced that John and Louise Falconer really *had* been framed, and that Frank Lindenauer was trying to murder Aiden and Meg to keep it a secret.

It wasn't too late to put a stop to this madness before the ultimate tragedy — the death of fifteen-year-old Aiden Falconer. But first Harris *had* to get through to this scared and bitter girl who had every reason to hate him.

"Margaret — *Meg* — I believe you, and that's the truth. We found a fingerprint proving that Frank Lindenauer is an alias for a man named Terence McKenzie. He's an ex-CIA operative with terrorist ties and a big beef against the government. I think he might have misled your parents into working for HORUS. Don't you see? Things are finally starting to work out for your family! But none of that's going to matter if Aiden gets killed. You have to trust me!"

"I'll trust you when Mom and Dad go free," she said stubbornly.

"The system doesn't work that way!" he pleaded. "I can't prove anything yet. But once you and your brother are safe, I'm sure — "

She swiveled away from him, staring stonily into the mountains of old court documents that had once sealed her parents' fate.

Harris wanted to howl his vexation through the halls of FBI Denver. She would never trust him. He had caused her family too much suffering.

He had to find another way to get her to give up her brother's location.

But how?

There are no new messages in your in-box.

Aiden stared at the sentence as if he believed he could change it through the force of his brain waves.

No new messages. No word from Frank Lindenauer.

It didn't make sense. This was a man who had pursued them relentlessly across thousands of miles. A man determined to see them dead.

Why would he stop now?

How many hours had Aiden tossed and turned, sleepless, praying for the terrifying bald assassin to leave them alone? Well, now it was happening —

Just when I need him to come after me!

Aiden's stomach churned, raw and painful. He was afraid of Hairless Frank, but he was even more afraid that the man had disappeared again, the way he had during Mom and Dad's trial. He was the only person on earth who could prove their innocence. It would be the end of all hope for John and Louise Falconer.

"Glad to see one of us has some earthly purpose for that idiot box."

At the sound of the farmer's voice, Aiden hurriedly exited the e-mail program.

Turnbull thumped up behind him on the crutches. "That's all there is to it? Fiddling with that little arrow thingamajig?"

Aiden tried to size up his employer. Had the man seen too much? There was no suspicion in the farmer's eyes — only the usual scorn he reserved for all things "newfangled."

"It's really easy, Mr. Turnbull. You just double-click on your browser" — he selected the Internet Explorer icon — "and choose where you'd like to go. You want to check the weather?"

"If I need to know the weather, I can stick my head out the window." The farmer raked him with gray, piercing eyes. "Is there something you want to tell me, Gary?"

Aiden stared back, trying to appear innocent, waiting for the ax to fall.

"I looked in the milk canister. Cows on strike or something?"

Aiden flushed deep red. With Meg gone, he was

the milker again. "I guess I have my good days and bad days," he offered lamely.

"Make sure tomorrow's a good day," the farmer said pointedly. "It's not healthy for the cows to be left like that."

"I'll do my best," Aiden promised, reflecting that if a message came in from Hairless Frank to meet him somewhere, the cows might have to milk themselves in the morning.

He stepped out onto the porch, nearly tripping over Turnbull's nail gun for the umpteenth time. He hugged himself against the chill. The nights had been growing cooler, but this was just plain cold. And — were those snow flurries?

Winter's coming.

It was a lame observation for most people. But for a fugitive, winter made survival impossibly more complicated. Shelter and warmth would no longer be for comfort; they would become absolute necessities. Coats, boots, hats, and gloves had to be considered. Walking, running, driving — everything would be harder on snow and ice.

There's no way Meg and I could have made it this far in January.

Meg. Her absence was a gaping hole in his heart. It seemed to Aiden that everything was falling apart

— their growing notoriety, Meg's betrayal, Hairless Frank's disappearance, the worsening weather . . .

Mom — Dad — what more can I do?

The hoofbeats were familiar now — a swelling drumroll coming from the direction of the pigsty. This would be the cherry on the bitter ice cream sundae: to be trampled by a prehistoric swine.

"No, Bernard!" he hissed. "It's just me — Gary! Stop!"

Into the cocoon of light surrounding the house exploded three hundred pounds of charging pig. Aiden held up his arms in a feeble attempt to fend off the attack. But this time, Bernard didn't run into him. Instead, he sped around Aiden in tight circles, grunting and breathing hard. Even Aiden, who was clueless about animals, could tell that the monster was jittery about something.

"What's the matter, Bernard? What's got you spooked?"

And then he saw it. Across the compound in the farmhand's apartment, a beam of light suddenly swept across the darkened window.

A flashlight.

Somebody was in there.

17

Frank Lindenauer! He must have followed us here.

The discovery was an adrenaline blast, radiating outward from Aiden's core. Somehow, the assassin had found him.

Aiden was astounded at the courage of his reaction. A professional killer was half a football field away, searching for him. Yet the rush he felt was not entirely one of terror. This was good news — Hairless Frank hadn't disappeared. He had just changed his strategy — setting a trap for Aiden instead of the other way around.

I should have expected it, Aiden told himself. *He's evil, not stupid.*

He struggled for calm. This was it — his chance to tape the confession that would clear his parents. The problem was that the recorder was on the nightstand inside the apartment — with Hairless Frank. By hook or by crook, he had to get to that

machine. That meant entering the apartment —
with an armed murderer inside.

I won't last three seconds!

He needed an equalizer. The pig? Bernard was
every bit as dangerous as any assassin, and twice the
size. Hairless Frank wouldn't be expecting an animal attack. Chances were, he'd be bowled over. By
the time he figured out what had happened to him,
Aiden would be in there with the tape recorder running.

"Come on, Bernard — let's get that guy!" He began to jog across the barnyard, the pig trotting by his
side, still snorting his agitation. Soon they were
standing just outside the closed door. He picked up
a pitchfork that was leaning against the wall of the
barn. It was no match for a nine-millimeter pistol.
But with any luck, Hairless Frank's gun would soon
be buried under three hundred pounds of pork.

A silent countdown: *Three, two, one* . . . He
reached in, swung the door wide, and stepped back
to let Bernard loose.

Bernard leaned his massive head inside, withdrew
it just as quickly, and stampeded off into the night,
leaving Aiden in front of the open doorway —

A perfect target!

Fear jolted him into action, and he dropped to the floor out of the line of fire. He couldn't see Hairless Frank, but that didn't mean the assassin wasn't there, hiding behind a chair, a table, waiting to start shooting. He crawled through the gloom, navigating by memory to the nightstand and the tape recorder.

Suddenly, a dark shape exploded out of the bathroom and made a beeline for the door. Aiden was caught off guard. He had expected an assault. Why was Hairless Frank running away?

Wildly, he swung his pitchfork at the shadowy figure. The assassin hurdled it and kept on going, fleeing out of the apartment into the barnyard.

"Come back — " Aiden croaked.

Wham!

The collision could be felt inside the apartment. One minute, Hairless Frank was sprinting across the lawn; the next, he was flying through the air. A second shape appeared, built like a Volkswagen. The squealing and grunting told the story. Bernard pounced on his prey, rooting and biting about the man's head and shoulders.

Aiden leaped to his feet in alarm. "Bernard — no! Back off! Don't hurt him!" If the huge animal accidentally killed Hairless Frank, then the evidence that would clear John and Louise Falconer would be lost forever.

Brandishing his pitchfork, he rushed over to the fallen intruder. The wave of bewildered disappointment almost took his breath away.

It was not Frank Lindenauer. The battered man beneath the pig's bulk was a lot thinner than the stocky assassin, with a full shock of blond hair.

"Who are you?" Aiden demanded.

"I'm Mike Delancey!" the victim panted as Bernard punished his face with a snout like a pile driver. "Call off your — what *is* this thing?"

"What were you doing in my apartment?" Aiden persisted, determined not to help until his questions had been answered.

"I'm a private investigator!"

"For who?"

"I work for Elias Holyfield."

All at once, Aiden understood. How many times had Mr. Turnbull talked about an army of snoops employed by the landlord? Who knew it would turn out to be true?

"Come on," Delancey quavered. "The pig's going to kill me!"

In spite of everything, Aiden felt a stab of compassion. He knew as well as anybody what it was like to be at this monster's mercy. "Back off, Bernard," he ordered. And when the animal didn't respond, he gave the snout a firm tap with the wooden handle of the pitchfork. The pig reversed a few paces, keeping its enraged eyes riveted on Delancey as the investigator got gingerly to his feet. The tight space of the apartment may not have been to Bernard's liking, but out here in the open, he was king of the barnyard.

"What does Holyfield want with me?" Aiden snapped.

"If you're gone, the farm isn't being worked," Delancey explained. "That's grounds for breaking the lease."

"Well, I'm not leaving," Aiden insisted. "Not for Holyfield, not for anybody!"

"Oh, yeah? I don't know who you are, kid, but something's not right with you." The investigator kept a nervous eye on the snarling Bernard as he challenged Aiden. "Where's the girl?"

"What girl?"

"I *saw* her," Delancey retorted. "You keep her under wraps, I'll give you that. She only comes out when Turnbull's not around. Who is she — your girlfriend?"

"I don't have to talk to you!" Aiden seethed. "You broke into my apartment. I could call the cops!"

The PI shrugged. "Suit yourself. I'd love to hear you explain yourself to the police. You're not from around here, but you've got no luggage and barely any clothes. It's like you're a homeless person. Or a runaway, more likely."

Aiden felt the fire of his upset frosting into icy panic. This man was a private investigator, trained in the art of seeking information. He was treading dangerously close to the truth about Aiden's identity.

"How'd you like me to sic Bernard on you again?" he threatened. "And this time, I won't call him off!"

Hearing its name, the pig emitted an unfriendly snort and advanced menacingly.

"Wait a minute — " The prospect of tangling with Bernard again was not appealing to Mike Delancey. "Listen, Mr. Holyfield's a reasonable man. He's got no beef with you. He just wants the right to sell his own land. That's why I'm authorized to offer you a thousand dollars cash to move on."

"And throw Mr. Turnbull to the sharks," Aiden added sourly.

"Growing season's over in a couple of weeks. A grand is more than Turnbull's paying you from now till then. Think of what you could do with that money — you and your lady friend."

Lady friend. The thought of Meg activated a heat source in Aiden's gut. There had once been a time when a thousand dollars would have made all the difference to the Falconers in their quest to exonerate their parents. It would have fed them, put a roof over their heads, bought them train and bus tickets. It would have kept them from risking their freedom, and sometimes their very lives, trespassing, stealing, and stowing away.

Money could never have changed the reality of their plight. But it might have made things a little easier, downgrading the 100 percent impossible to merely 98 percent. And that was no small difference with the entire family on the line. It might even have made it worth betraying Mr. Turnbull who, despite his oddness, was turning out to be a pretty nice guy.

But now, with Meg gone and Hairless Frank dropped from sight, their quest was in ruins. A thousand dollars wouldn't change that. Neither would a million.

Aiden tried out a nasty look copied from the face

of Hairless Frank himself. "You've got thirty seconds to get off Zephraim Turnbull's farm. Then I'm sending Bernard after you."

Delancey raised his arms in a gesture of surrender. "Okay, okay, I'm gone. I'm just asking you to think about it, that's all. Let me talk to Mr. Holyfield. What if we double it? Two thousand bucks?"

"Twenty seconds," said Aiden evenly.

The private investigator turned and ran.

It was not until Aiden heard the sound of the car door and the motor starting up that he allowed himself to breathe again.

18

The hotel room was standard economy-class drab. But to Meg, after months on the run, it screamed of luxury. She had slept in a hayloft, a boxcar, and a steel drum. Real beds had been few and far between.

The only feature not to her liking was the connecting door to the next room. That, she knew, was home to all six feet seven inches of Emmanuel Harris. He was staying close by to keep an eye on her — like ten straight hours of interrogation hadn't been enough!

The agent couldn't seem to get it through his thick skull that she had nothing to tell him. Not until she knew the details of Aiden's one-on-one with Hairless Frank. Only then would she inform Harris so the FBI could crash the meeting and rescue her brother.

Such split-second timing in a life-and-death matter was nerve-racking, but there was no other way.

If she spilled the beans about Aiden's location now, Harris would head straight to the farm to arrest him. Risky as it was, Aiden had to have the chance to trick a confession out of Hairless Frank before the FBI swooped down on the whole thing.

She frowned. Getting in touch with Aiden wasn't going to be easy. There was no phone in the hired hand's apartment — which left her two options. She could either call Mr. Turnbull's house and ask the farmer if she could speak to Gary Graham . . . or, if she could somehow get her hands on a computer, she could e-mail falx@zipnet.usa.

She sighed heavily. Not much chance of doing either, not with her roommate standing guard.

Agent Lucy Batista, FBI Denver, had been assigned by Harris to stick to Meg like glue, never letting the girl out of her sight. Meg remembered overhearing Harris's instructions to his agent: "She's got a face like an angel, but don't you believe it. This kid has made monkeys out of more cops than you could fit in the Rose Bowl, starting with me. Don't leave her alone for a second. If she talks in her sleep, I want to know what she says."

"You don't have to worry," Meg told her jailer. "I'm not going anywhere. I wouldn't have given myself up if I wasn't ready to be in custody."

Agent Batista looked at her sympathetically. "I know, sweetie, but — "

"I'm not your sweetie!" Meg cut her off, bristling over every inch of her body. "What do you think this is — a slumber party? Do you have any idea what's happened to me and my family?"

Batista was apologetic. "Of course I know. Everybody knows. I was just trying to explain why I can't leave you alone. It's not that I don't trust you. It's FBI policy."

Yet an hour later, after the two had watched *American Idol* on TV, Lucy Batista yawned her way into the bathroom to take a shower.

Meg couldn't believe it. Had FBI policy changed during *American Idol*? What had happened to *I can't leave you alone*?

Of course she knew there was a guard outside the door. So she would be stopped if she tried to run out. But here she was, by herself in the room, with the total run of the place!

She made a beeline for the phone on the nightstand, but froze partway there. Her eyes fell on Agent Batista's laptop computer. It sat on the desk, fully booted up, the power light flashing in standby mode.

Meg pounced on it. E-mail was the only way to

get straight through to Aiden. She opened Outlook Express and typed in the address falx@zipnet.usa.

> Aiden — Don't freak out. I haven't deserted you. Just tell me where and when the meeting is going to happen. I'll be there.

She paused. Communicating with Aiden had proved to be possible. Having him reply was another matter altogether.

But, she reasoned, *when the meeting with Hairless Frank is all set, it won't matter if the FBI intercepts the message. Then it'll be time to tell Harris anyway.*

She turned back to the keyboard and added:

> URGENT! Don't reply until you have all the details! Can't explain now. You'll have to trust me.

She sat back. How to sign off? It was a dumb thing to get hung up on at a time like this. And yet —

If Aiden's plan didn't go well, if the cavalry was half a minute late getting to the scene — well, then, these might be the last sentences she would ever direct toward her brother.

All at once, the pressure of finding the right words, the perfect words, caught in her throat, and she sat there, paralyzed.

With a clunk of the plumbing, the shower was shut off, and the curtain swished back on its rings. In a few seconds, Agent Batista would be upon her.

Fingers flying, Meg sent the e-mail and removed any record of it from both the sent items and the deleted file. She shut down the program and closed the lid, putting the laptop back in standby mode. She was on her bed when Batista emerged from the bathroom, wrapped in a terry-cloth robe.

"Everything okay here, Meg?"

Meg didn't answer, and it was not out of rudeness. Her mind still reeled with the things she could have written to her brother. And the fact that the right words, whatever they were, might now remain forever unsaid.

At the Hash House, a tiny roadside luncheonette seven miles east of the Turnbull farm, the lone customer was tying into a big feed of pork chops.

The counterman was looking pointedly at his watch. It was already half an hour past usual closing. "Pretty late for a heavy meal," he commented.

"A pig almost ate me tonight," said private investigator Mike Delancey, mouth full, "and I'm return-ing the favor."

"Fair enough," said the cook without much inter-est. He began sponging the counter, hoping that his customer would finish up and go home.

Delancey just sat there, chewing and savoring. He wondered how many pork chops would come off a creature like Bernard. Enough to feed a battalion, probably. What an experience! He was still feeling shaky. And the embarrassment of running away like a scared rabbit really rankled.

That lousy kid, that Gary — it would be nice to get even with him. Something was not quite right about him anyway. For starters, no way was he eighteen years old. Sixteen would be a stretch. And he was definitely lying about the girl. Delancey had seen her with his own eyes. Runaways, probably — a couple of rich kids who thought it was cool to hide out on the Turnbull farm.

Mr. Holyfield would be very grateful if Gary Gra-ham was removed from the scene. But going to the police again wasn't an option — at least not un-til Delancey knew more about the kid. The cops wouldn't arrest somebody for not having luggage.

What else did he know about Gary Graham? His accent was hard to place, but it was definitely East

Coast — that would support the runaway theory. And the truth was his face looked kind of familiar. Maybe that was just because he'd been watching the kid for days. After all, how would a Colorado PI recognize an East Coast runaway and his girlfriend — or at least, *some* girl. Who else could she be? His sister?

For the second time that night, pork threatened the life of Mike Delancey. He began to choke. The cook leaned across the counter and pounded him on the back.

"You okay, mister?"

When he got his breath back, Delancey had to admit that he was better than okay. He'd been hired to do Holyfield's dirty work and, in the process, he had stumbled on twenty-five thousand dollars in reward money. Courtesy of Gary Graham, aka Aiden Falconer.

19

Meg lay on her bed, still fully clothed, dead asleep. Her day had begun at four o'clock in the morning and had been endless and stressful. She had passed out from the sheer weight of her exhaustion and emotional upset.

Agent Lucy Batista stepped through the connecting door into Emmanuel Harris's room. "She's dead to the world, poor kid," she reported. "Did we get it?"

Harris nodded, swiveling his laptop so she could see it. There on the screen was the text of Meg's recent e-mail to her brother. "Our tech people caught it. They're in touch with the Internet service provider to get the location of the recipient."

Agent Batista squinted at the message. "What meeting? Between her brother and the man they call Lindenauer?"

"That's my guess," Harris nodded grimly. "Or at

least she believes that's what Aiden has in mind. For sure, it's the reason she gave herself up."

"Or she's conning us," Batista added thoughtfully.

"It wouldn't be the first time," Harris conceded wearily. "But I don't think so."

His cell phone rang. It was the FBI's tech center in Washington, DC — a conference call with the offices of <u>Zipnet.USA.</u>

"Conference call?" Harris repeated. "What for? We need an address, period."

"They won't release the information to us," the tech explained. "They're asking for the authorization of the agent in the field."

Harris reeled off his name and badge number . . . and a lot more as well. "What's the matter with you people? Why are you wasting my time?"

The Zipnet representative was apologetic but firm. "I'm sorry, Agent Harris, but it's company policy to double-check because of the other inquiry."

Harris was on his feet. "Other inquiry?"

"About an hour ago," the man confirmed. "Another agent called for a street address on this very account."

Harris was horrified. "And you gave it to him?"

"He was from the FBI!"

"*I'm* from the FBI! You just released private information to someone who may very well be a murderer! I need that address — *now!*"

On a piece of hotel stationery, he wrote:

Zephraim Turnbull, RR #6, Aberdeen, CO

The next thing Meg knew, she was being hauled out of bed by strong arms. Her eyes came to bleary focus on Emmanuel Harris, yelling at her from point-blank range. What was he saying?

"You've got to take us to Aiden! *Now!*"

"Put me down!" she demanded in outrage.

A piece of paper was held under her nose. On it was Zephraim Turnbull's name and address.

In spite of her shock, she tried to bluff her way through. "Never heard of him."

"Look," said Harris, "I'm going to find it eventually. But only after wandering down every dark country road in Aberdeen. How'd you like it if Frank Lindenauer got there first?"

"You're bluffing!" she accused. "Frank Lindenauer doesn't know anything!"

"Are you willing to bet your brother's life on that? I just traced your e-mail. And Zipnet says somebody performed the identical trace an hour ago. Who do you think that might be?"

In that instant, Meg's defenses crumbled, and she very nearly went down with them. This was her worst-case scenario — being too late to save her brother.

Hairless Frank had gone after Aiden already. The killer had a head start. The "meeting" was about to happen, right on the Turnbull farm. And Aiden had no idea it was coming.

She turned to the man who had arrested her parents, the man she hated above all others.

"I'll take you there."

In the dead of night, the Turnbull farm was as dark as intergalactic space. A single flashlight bobbed along the edge of the pasture adjoining the barnyard. Aiden trudged the path, leading one of the cows, Essie. Or possibly Babette. Even after all this time, he had trouble telling the two apart.

Yes, it was insanity to be milking a cow at midnight — especially when the whole world seemed to be falling apart. But what else was he going to do? In the state he was in, sleep wasn't really an option. With all his worries — Meg gone, no word from Hairless Frank, and now a spy from Holyfield on his neck — the least he could do was his job. He owed it to Mr. Turnbull. He even sort of owed it to the cows.

So Essie (Babette?) was the test cow. He was going to get milk from her, or die trying. And if that worked, he would bring in the others, one by one. It was going to be a long night.

Am I losing my mind?

He had no answer to that question. But doing something, even milking, was better than having time to think when all thoughts were so awful.

He opened the creaking door and reached up to pull the chain that lit the single bulb in the hanging pigtail socket. Light flooded the barn. He set up the pail and stool, and led Essie into the milking stall.

"Okay, girl," he said aloud. "Here goes." He grabbed hold with what he hoped was authority, and began moving his hands in a pistonlike motion, the way Meg always did it. To his surprise, the result was not bad at all. Thin streams of milk sang against the metal of the empty bucket. He broke into a goofy grin of triumph.

Essie was not as elated by the victory. She had been asleep in the field and would have preferred to remain that way until daybreak. Her head swiveled around, and she glared at him with a loud moo of complaint.

Aiden ignored her and milked doggedly on. But when he saw the telltale twitch in the animal's haunch, he knew exactly what was coming. The hoof came up, aimed unerringly at his head. Hugging the bucket to protect the milk, Aiden ducked off the stool and made himself small on the straw-covered floor.

The kick missed him.

So did the bullet.

The shot came from the doorway, whizzing barely an inch away from his shoulder and burying itself in a wooden post. There was no doubt in Aiden's mind that its path was straight through the empty space where his head had been a split second before.

As he rolled, he caught a glimpse of the figure with the gun standing just inside the barn — the stocky frame, the burning eyes, the bald head.

Hairless Frank.

The assassin had an overwhelming advantage — gun against bare hands, professional against rank amateur, in a small, enclosed space.

Pure instinct took over. Aiden grabbed the milking stool and flung it up at the pigtail socket. The bulb shattered with a pop, and the barn was plunged into darkness.

Hairless Frank couldn't shoot what he couldn't see!

Now, how am I going to get out of here?

Zephraim Turnbull was in the last place he had ever expected himself to be — sitting in front of that fool computer and actually using the blasted thing.

He had to give Gary credit. There really was a whole world inside this cockamamie invention. And the farmhand had painstakingly showed him exactly how to access it.

Access it. Listen to that. He was throwing around computer language already. He had even found an online article about Mountain View Homes and their plans to develop this area. A map actually showed the new subdivision running right through his farm! The nerve of that Holyfield, promising Mountain View the Turnbull farm to build on. It was unbelievable! Yet there it was, right on the *Denver Chronicle*'s Web site.

He scrolled down, skimming the paper for articles of interest. And then a picture caught his eye.

Under the small caption STILL AT LARGE, was a photograph of — he blinked —

Gary, his hired man!

Denver police still have no leads pointing to the whereabouts of Aiden and Margaret Falconer, the children of convicted traitors John and Louise Falconer . . .

Even the unflappable Zephraim Turnbull was rocked back on his heels. The Falconer kids! Gary was Aiden Falconer! And the sister — he thought back to the mysterious girl Holyfield was always bleating about.

Two fugitives from justice were lamming it on his farm!

At that very moment, an unmistakable sound cracked across his barnyard. It would have taken a great deal to distract him from the huge discovery he had just made, but this did the trick.

It was a pistol shot.

20

A cold, raspy voice rang out in the pitch-black of the barn. "Okay, kid, you wanted to talk. Here I am."

"First you drop that gun!" Aiden blurted, and was instantly sorry. Hairless Frank aimed in the direction of the words and fired. Aiden saw the muzzle flash and heard the slug rip into the wall not far away.

He's shooting at the sound! The realization amped his panic to a new level. How could he get out of here if every move created noise, and every noise was a target?

Luckily, the shots had agitated Essie, who was thrashing about and mooing her distress. It covered the rustling of Aiden slithering on his belly through the straw into the second stall. His hand closed on the milk pail he'd known he would find there. It was a risky move, but one he had to chance. His only hope was to draw the assassin away from the lone exit.

His reared his arm back and heaved the pail toward the back of the barn, where the milk canisters were stored. It struck with a clatter. A volley of shots added to the din. Flash after flash illuminated Hairless Frank's monstrous silhouette.

Aiden's heart sank. His enemy was still in front of the doorway. Of course — Hairless Frank was a professional. He would never allow himself to be lured away from the position of power.

As long as he's blocking the exit, I'll never get out of here. Unless —

It came to Aiden like a distant point of light in an endless tunnel. The barn had some rotting wood right at ground level on the outside wall. Mr. Turnbull was planning to replace those boards as soon as he was finished with the porch. If Aiden could find the right spot, maybe it was weak enough for him to —

He squirmed to the back of the stall and ran his hand over the planks. The wood was damp and crumbly, but there was no give to it.

"Pack it in, kid," the assassin advised. "You've got nowhere to run."

Aiden rolled under the barrier separating stall two from three. The sound of his movement brought a bullet thudding into the divider. Barely daring to breathe, he pawed the wall. This was the spot! There were holes big enough to poke his finger through. The wood was weak . . . but was it weak enough?

Praying that Essie's renewed mooing would cover his activity, he turned onto his back, swiveled, and aimed both work boots at the wall. Then he pulled back his legs and dealt a mighty kick to the rotted boards. The wood splintered, opening a hole to the outside. He pounded with both feet, and the ruined planks came apart.

Just a little more —

A bullet chirped past his ear, very close. He'd hoped for a bigger hole. But what were scrapes and splinters compared to the horror that awaited him inside the barn?

He squeezed through the opening, barely noticing the sharp, splintered wood ripping at his flesh. Then he was sprinting, intent only on flight — until the thought struck him.

The tape recorder! Get the tape recorder!

The idea of confronting Hairless Frank once more after just barely escaping with his life turned his heart over.

You can't run away! You have to get his confession!

He came to an abrupt stop, quivering like a hunting dog on the scent. The tape recorder was in the hired hand's quarters! He took a step in the direction of his apartment.

The tackle from behind flattened him to the ground. Aiden rolled over onto his back, expecting to see Frank Lindenauer's pistol about to deliver the shot that would be the last thing he would ever hear.

Instead, a handcuff clicked onto his wrist and pulled painfully tight. Mike Delancey snapped the other cuff onto his own arm and hauled Aiden upright.

"Hi, kid," he said smugly. "Miss me?"

"Let me go!" Aiden hissed. "There's a guy trying to kill me!"

"You're very convincing," Delancey conceded. "I can see how you kept ahead of the cops all these weeks, you and your sister."

Aiden stared at the private investigator. Delancey knew who he was! But at this terrible moment, that fact was low on Aiden's list of priorities.

"It's no lie!" he pleaded. "There's a guy with a gun in that barn! When he figures out I'm not in there, he's going to come out after me!"

"You must think I'm some dumb flatfoot!" Delancey sneered. "You're worth twenty-five grand!"

He jerked on the cuffs, hauling his captive along. "You're coming with me!"

Aiden stumbled along behind him. "Please! I'll go with you! I'll let you turn me in for the money! But *not now*!"

Delancey snorted and kept going.

All at once, Aiden's desperation morphed into white-hot rage. Mom and Dad would not spend the rest of their lives in prison because of this bozo's greed.

"You better let me go," he seethed, "or I'm calling Bernard!" And when Delancey kept on dragging him, Aiden knew he had to follow through. Yes, it was dangerous to make noise with Hairless Frank so close by. But there was no other way.

He placed two fingers of his free hand inside his mouth and whistled long and loud. That was how Mr. Turnbull summoned his guard pig. But would it work for Aiden?

Delancey looked at him nervously. "Nice try, Falconer. Like a pig comes when you call him."

Then they heard the hoofbeats.

In the space of a split second, Mike Delancey asked himself if twenty-five thousand dollars was worth another meeting with Bernard. When the handcuff key came out of his pocket, the private investigator's hand was shaking so badly that Aiden had to take charge and unlock himself. The instant the two were separated, Delancey fled for his car.

Keeping a wary eye out for the pig, Aiden started back for the apartment and his tape recorder.

The squeak and slap of the screen door of the farmhouse stopped him in his tracks. He turned to see Zephraim Turnbull limp onto the porch, on one crutch only. In the other hand was a double-barreled shotgun.

Aiden was stricken. If Hairless Frank came out of that barn and saw an armed man, he'd blow him away without a thought!

It was Aiden's fault that Mr. Turnbull was in peril of his life —

I've got to warn him!

21

Hunched over the wheel, his head pressed against the roof of the small rental car, Agent Harris was becoming frustrated. "Well, is this the road, or isn't it?"

"I can't tell!" Meg yelled, her indecision bubbling into belligerence. "It's too dark!"

"Focus on the landmarks," Agent Batista advised soothingly. "The barns, the houses, maybe a distinctive silo."

"I was stuck inside all the time!" Meg snapped back. "I wasn't mapping the neighborhood!"

She was so angry with herself that she could barely think straight. A killer was closing in on Aiden. He might be there already! And here she was, unable to get her act together, dithering around like — like — like Aiden would!

Concentrate! she commanded herself.

A tiny bend in the road brought the car's headlights down a long double-rut driveway. It was only for a second, but the beams played off the tailgate of Zephraim Turnbull's pickup truck.

"Right there!" she screamed.

"*Where?*"

"You passed it! That driveway!"

Harris threw the car into reverse.

Frank Lindenauer made his silent way across the barnyard, alert to any sound and movement. His muscular body trembled with rage. He was a professional — he knew emotion was a weakness that could blunt his skill. Yet his fury was difficult to contain.

How long had he stood alone in the barn, straining to hear sounds of movement over the caterwauling of that cow? He had been guarding the only exit, and yet Aiden Falconer had made it out of there.

He had badly underestimated the Falconer children. He knew that now. They were formidable enemies. But that was all going to change in short order tonight.

He tensed like a raptor sensing its prey. Someone was out there, cutting across the barnyard toward the road. Someone in a hurry. He moved stealthily to intercept, adjusting his sight to detect motion in the dark.

He sprang, grabbing the fleeing figure in a choke hold, cutting off any cry for help. He pressed his pistol against a sweaty temple.

"Where's your sister?"

A completely terrified voice quavered, "Don't shoot — you've got the wrong guy!"

The assassin spun his prisoner around. "Who are you?"

Mike Delancey was almost witless to discover that Aiden had been telling the truth about a killer running loose on the property. "I'm nobody!" he babbled. "I swear!"

"Where's Aiden Falconer?"

"He was heading for the house — "

Savagely, Hairless Frank brought the butt of his gun down on the private investigator's head. The man dropped like a stone, unconscious.

The assassin turned his attention to the residence.

It would all end there.

Aiden pounded onto the porch where the farmer stood armed and ready.

"Mr. Turnbull, get back inside! Somebody's after me!"

Turnbull steadied himself on his single crutch. "If you think I'm going to let that snake Holyfield — "

"It isn't Holyfield!" Aiden insisted. "It's a professional killer! You don't know who I am!"

The farmer hefted his shotgun. "I know exactly who you are. And nobody's going to hurt you — not on *my* watch!"

At that very instant, Agent Emmanuel Harris burst out of the darkness, pounding toward them in a full sprint, weapon at the ready.

To Zephraim Turnbull's eyes, this was a killer if there ever was one. The farmer took aim and fired.

The blast drowned out Aiden's demented "*No-o-o-o-o!*" and knocked the big FBI agent flat on his back on the turf. He lay there, unmoving.

Aiden was practically hysterical. "That's not the right guy! You just shot a federal agent!"

"Drop it!" Agent Lucy Batista leaped onto the porch, pistol in one hand, ID in the other.

The farmer leaned his shotgun against the porch rail and backed off meekly. Batista snatched the weapon and jumped down to kneel over the fallen Harris. She pulled out her cell phone, activating the walkie-talkie function. "I've got an agent down in Aberdeen off Rural Route 6! I need an ambulance *pronto*!"

A smaller figure appeared beside her and bent over the fallen FBI agent.

A cry was torn from Aiden's throat. "Meg!" He took a step toward his sister.

Like a serpent from the shadows, a black-clad arm wrapped around Meg's midsection, hauling her upright and pulling her away from Harris and Batista.

Batista reacted instantly, swinging her pistol around and training it on the attacker. But by then, Hairless Frank had Meg in a headlock and was pressing the barrel of his gun to her ear.

"Let her go!" Batista ordered.

The assassin's voice was steady, measured. "Stay back or she dies."

Aiden started forward, but the FBI agent froze him with a bark of "Stop!" He realized in a flood of horror that there was absolutely nothing he could do. Frank Lindenauer was outnumbered, yet *he* was the one in control. The slightest twitch of his index finger and Meg's life was over.

For the Falconers, it was the ultimate nightmare — to be at the utter mercy of the man who wanted them dead.

22

Batista tried to reason with Hairless Frank. "You can't win this. I've got backup on the way."

The assassin was unmoved. "Don't push me. I hold the only card that matters, and we both know it. Here's the plan — I'm going to walk right out of this, and you're going to let me."

"Leave the girl with us," Batista tried to bargain.

"Don't insult my intelligence." The killer grinned, a smile that did not extend to his ice-cold eyes. "Don't worry — I'll take good care of her."

"No!" Aiden shouted.

"Mind your own business, kid!" Hairless Frank advised harshly. "You've had a nice run, and I've got the scars to prove it. But you never really had a chance."

Aiden would not back down. "You're not taking my sister!"

The assassin gestured in Batista's direction. "You

think this fed will let me get thirty feet without a hostage?"

"You'll still have a hostage," Aiden argued. "Me."

The agent stared at him, although her weapon remained on its target. "Stay out of this, Aiden! You don't know what you're saying!"

Aiden ignored her, directing his words at Hairless Frank. "We'll do a switch. Meg goes free. I come with you."

For the first time in the standoff, Meg spoke up. With the assassin's bear-trap grip on her neck, her voice was barely a terrified quaver. But her message was classic Meg — brave, strong, and not open to negotiation: "Forget it!"

Hairless Frank laughed — a mirthless chuckle that chilled Aiden to his trembling core. "You Falconers are such a bunch of do-gooders! Maybe I should let you each fight it out for the privilege of sacrificing yourself to protect the other one. Just like your parents — what a couple of Boy Scouts! Do you know how easy it was to sucker two college professors into working for HORUS? When I told them I was CIA, and they'd be helping their country, they were like puppy dogs, eager to do anything

I asked." He snorted in disgust. "Patriotism is a pathetic emotion. It makes you weak and stupid."

He began to back away, pulling Meg along with him.

"Don't move!" ordered Batista. Her pistol arm was as rigid as a steel rod.

"Go ahead — shoot," Hairless Frank invited coolly. "Even if you do hit me and not the girl, what are the chances that I won't squeeze the trigger?"

"Don't let them go!" piped Aiden. "As soon as he's out of range, he'll kill her!"

"Nobody's going anywhere!" insisted Batista, not quite as confidently.

But Hairless Frank sensed his advantage and continued to press it — retreating with careful baby steps.

"That's far enough!" Batista exclaimed.

Aiden watched the standoff, appalled. How could he allow his sister to be carried off and murdered? Yet what could he do to prevent it? If the FBI couldn't handle Hairless Frank, what chance did a fifteen-year-old kid have against this irresistible force of nature?

Drowning in dread, he didn't hear the rumble of hoofbeats until it was too late.

Bernard burst out of the surrounding darkness, three hundred pounds of charging livestock in a state of high agitation.

Zephraim Turnbull spotted the guard pig first. "Bernard — *no!*"

Bernard tried to stop, but he had too much momentum. The animal careened into their midst, narrowly avoiding the prostrate body of Emmanuel Harris. A meaty flank collided with Agent Batista, sending her sprawling to the grass.

Aiden experienced a jolt of electricity as if he'd taken a direct hit from a lightning bolt. With Batista out of the picture —

There's nothing to keep Hairless Frank from killing Meg!

There was no time for words, or even thought. It was pure instinct. Aiden flung himself across the porch, arms outstretched in a desperate grab for the object he hoped would be where he remembered it. He felt the nail gun in his hands, pointed it at Hairless Frank, and fired.

The crack hurt his ears. The recoil tossed the power tool from his grasp and knocked him flat on his back.

The nail tore into the assassin's leg just above the

knee. With a cry of shock and pain, Hairless Frank grasped his thigh, releasing the headlock that imprisoned Meg.

Meg dove for freedom. She hit the ground and scrambled on all fours in an attempt to put as much distance as possible between herself and the killer as he wheeled furiously around to fire the shot that would end Meg's life. The sharp report of a pistol rang out.

Aiden gawked through tears of grief. His sister was still *moving*, crawling madly away from her captor. Then Aiden's eyes found Agent Batista. She was up on one knee, her smoking gun leveled at the assassin. An expression of stunned disbelief was frozen on Hairless Frank's face. A crimson bloodstain had appeared on his shirt.

As if in slow motion, the stocky, powerful frame of the traitor Frank Lindenauer crumpled to the turf of the barnyard.

Meg sprang up and threw herself at her brother, seizing him by the collar. "Did you get it? You got it, right?"

"*She* got him," Aiden replied, indicating Batista. "He's dead."

"No — his confession!" she gasped. "The tape recorder! You were right! He said it all —

everything about how he framed Mom and Dad!"

The color drained from Aiden's face, leaving him white and shaking. In the heat of the standoff, with Meg so close to death, the tape recorder had been the last thing on his mind.

"No," he said finally. "I couldn't get to it."

The agony on his sister's face was a knife in his heart. "But he's *dead*!" she wailed. "He won't ever be able to say it again!"

Throughout these horrendous weeks on the run, the Falconers had never known a moment of such complete despair. No matter how great their suffering, how terrifying their circumstances, there had always been hope — the chance, however slight, that they might one day help their parents. Now that chance lay dead at their feet.

The words that would have saved John and Louise Falconer were now nothing but smoke in the wind.

They fell toward each other and clung together, too devastated to be aware of anything but their sorrow. There were no words, no tears. Aiden and Meg were completely empty. They had given every atom of their existence to this quest, and it had not been enough.

Sirens heralded the approach of the ambulance.

Tires crunched on the dirt drive — FBI backup, local police. Aiden and Meg noticed none of it. Any chance of getting their lives back had been destroyed with Frank Lindenauer.

Mom and Dad would remain in prison for the rest of their natural lives.

The Falconer family was over.

23

Jail.

They were right back where they'd started.

No, worse than that, Meg decided bitterly. Sunnydale Farm had been a minimum-security detention center. She and Aiden had loathed it.

It was Disney World compared to here.

There was nothing minimum about the Danforth Juvenile Correctional Facility outside Roanoke, Virginia. There were high stone walls and fences with razor wire. Searchlight towers ringed the perimeter. And the guards weren't called supervisors or counselors or teachers. They were guards and they were armed.

It had all happened so fast after the showdown on the Turnbull farm. She and Aiden had been bounced from the FBI to the Denver police to the Department of Juvenile Corrections with dizzying speed. Deputy Director Adler himself had come all the way from Washington to escort them to Dan-forth.

Meg would never forget his cold words as the car had approached the forbidding gray ramparts of this place of no hope: "You're not going to burn *this* one down."

Back then the shock was still so fresh, the horror at the failure of their quest so painful, that all they could do was repeat the obvious questions: *When can we talk to our parents? When can we call our lawyers? Why are we being locked up without a trial?*

"If I were you two," was Adler's acid response, "I wouldn't be asking for favors. You destroyed one of our facilities. And the cost in manpower to chase you down could have run a small country for a year. Excuse me for not just turning you loose until trial. I guess I'm not the trusting type."

Trial. They had lived through their parents' trial. Now it would be their turn.

Meg dreaded hearing the charges read out in open court. They had broken so many laws in their efforts to stay free so they could track down Frank Lindenauer. No one would ever understand how hard they'd worked to minimize their crimes, to steal as little as possible, and only when they'd had no choice. No one would believe how they'd made mental notes to someday pay back what they owed.

Worst of all, no one would ever see that they had done it all in pursuit of justice for their poor parents. There would never be justice now. Any chance of it had died with Hairless Frank. Agent Batista and Zephraim Turnbull had heard Lindenauer's confession. But in the heat of a life-and-death moment, words could be confused, misunderstood, forgotten. Whatever the reason, it had not been enough.

It's almost like Mom and Dad really are guilty, because there's no way to prove it isn't true.

She and Aiden would no doubt be found guilty, too. They were Falconers, fruit of the traitorous tree. They had to be locked away for the good of society.

For how long? She could not even hazard a melancholy guess. And once they got out — what future would they have then? No family, their name reviled. That was the craziest part. They were in maximum security. But, terrible as it was, Meg didn't have the slightest desire to escape. Not now, with no hope for their parents, no quest to follow.

Nothing to escape to.

The one person who might have been persuaded to believe them was the architect of all their misfortunes, Agent Emmanuel Harris. Meg had no way of knowing, but she suspected Harris was probably dead. He had neither moved nor uttered a sound since Turnbull had shot him down.

That was another disaster. The farmer, who had only been trying to protect Aiden, was probably in jail for killing an FBI agent. He would lose his farm to Holyfield after all.

Everything the Falconers touched turned to mud.

As awful as she felt for herself and her parents, what really worried her was Aiden. Meg was angry and bitter and depressed. She would find herself crying in her cell one minute; the next, she might be clawing the bars in a blind fury.

Aiden showed none of these emotions. He was like a zombie. She only saw him in the afternoon in the exercise yard, and they were separated by a chain-link fence. But each day, he seemed a little more distant and withdrawn. Like Meg, he had devoted his entire soul to proving their parents' innocence. Now that the quest was gone, he had no soul.

He was an empty shell.

Aiden was ready to lie down and die — but Miguel Reyes wouldn't let him.

Miguel had been with the Falconers at Sunnydale. They had run together from Nebraska all the way to Vermont. Miguel had been recaptured there and had been in Danforth ever since.

"This is hard time, yo," he told Aiden. "The guards are nasty mean, and I got nothing good to say about the class of people in here."

In his opinion, the one positive thing that had happened to him was that Aiden — his best friend in the world — had turned up in the very same cell block.

Aiden didn't point out that he and Miguel had never been friends. They had, in fact, been pretty close to enemies. But Aiden was glad to know somebody — somebody streetwise and tough — in this very scary place.

There were convicted murderers in the facility, armed robbers, and gang members galore. Violence was an everyday occurrence. There would be a sudden outbreak of shouting, and pretty soon somebody was being hauled off to the hospital wing, bloody and beaten.

These were not just fistfights. There were homemade weapons here — knives, shanks, clubs.

"Should have stayed put at Sunnydale, yo," was

Miguel's opinion. "This is no place for you and your little sis."

Every time Aiden thought of Meg in this hideous lockup, his depression grew blacker.

At first, he had barely dared to breathe for fear of drawing the attention of his dangerous fellow inmates. He drew their attention anyway. The prison population had been following news coverage of the Falconer fugitives — and cheering as the brother and sister left hordes of frustrated police officers in their wake.

On day one, he'd walked into the mess hall to a standing ovation. He was a hero — for now. But how long would that last? He was younger than most, and weaker than all. Even with Miguel's help, he couldn't see himself surviving here.

It's no more than I deserve, he reminded himself listlessly. This was all his fault. *If I had found a way to get to the tape recorder, everything would be different.*

He had blown their only chance.

"You got to pull yourself together, Falcon," was Miguel's advice. "Place like this — the sharks smell blood in the water a mile away. You don't want it to be yours."

"Maybe I've got it coming," Aiden told him.

* * *

There were school classes at Danforth, but they were a joke. No one — neither teachers nor students — believed any of the inmates would have a use for education. These were lifetime criminals. Most would graduate to adult prison at the age of eighteen.

There was no future here. In that way, Aiden fit in perfectly.

The largest portion of each day was spent on work detail.

"That's how they keep down the violence," Miguel explained as they trudged through the main gate, rakes on their shoulders. "Work you so hard you've got no strength left for beating on people."

Which was fine with Aiden. Exhaustion was what he craved — anything to make him too tired to feel.

That's a plus when your only feelings are misery and dispair.

Today's job was both backbreaking and mind-numbing. The crew was required to rake leaves from the six-mile stretch of road that linked Danforth with the interstate.

If the workers harbored any thoughts of escape during these trips outside the walls, the guards were carrying high-powered rifles. Badges on their uniforms proclaimed them to be expert marksmen.

Aiden never even considered running. With the evidence that would clear John and Louise Falconer forever out of reach, even freedom seemed pointless.

They worked for five hours with only a twenty-minute lunch break, and started back just before four P.M. The procession was a quarter mile from the prison when they began to hear strident shouts. As they drew closer, they could see a car stopped at the main gate. The hubbub of voices resolved itself into the urgent rhythm of a heated argument.

"Hold up!" called one of the work detail guards.

Aiden squinted at the group of people gathered at the sentry hut. He recognized the warden himself there, and two other officials from the prison office. Everyone else was in uniform, except —

The rake dropped from Aiden's hand with a clatter. It was the last person he had ever expected to see again. A familiar silhouette straightened up to tower over the other men.

Agent Emmanuel Harris — alive!

24

One arm was in a sling, but otherwise Harris seemed unhurt. And he was furious, as usual, waving a manila envelope and bellowing, "My authority beats your authority! You never *had* any authority — not over my prisoners!" He turned and caught sight of the work crew. "There's one of them now!"

It was amazing. The warden of Danforth was the king of that tight little world. Yet all it took was a few documents from the envelope. On the spot, Aiden was released into Harris's custody, and Meg was brought from the girls' wing and given over as well.

Meg gawked at the six-foot-seven agent. "But — but you're dead!" she blurted.

His expression was unreadable. "Disappointed?"

She glared back at him. "No."

Aiden was surprised at the degree of his relief at the sight of Harris alive. So many horrible things

had happened. One less casualty had to be a plus —
even if it was J. Edgar Giraffe.

The Falconers were handcuffed together and
then handcuffed again to the inside of the rear doors
of Harris's rental car. The FBI man started up the
engine.

The warden was still protesting. "Deputy Director Adler brought me these prisoners personally."

"Adler is the idiot who put those kids on a prison
farm in the first place," Harris growled. "Why
should I be surprised that he did something even
stupider this time?"

They roared off toward the interstate.

"Where are you taking us?" Aiden demanded.

"You two have been calling the shots for a long
time," Harris said grimly. "Now it's my turn. Just sit
tight and keep quiet. You'll find out soon enough."

Aiden and Meg exchanged nervous glances. What
was J. Edgar Giraffe up to? Where were they going? Were they being transferred someplace even
worse than Danforth? Aiden couldn't imagine what
that might be. But hard experience had taught him
there was no limit to the misfortune that could be
heaped on anyone named Falconer.

In the backseat, the siblings huddled together for
strength and comfort. No words passed between

them. They did not want to give Harris the satisfaction of hearing their thoughts. Both knew that this ghastly misadventure was about to take yet another sudden turn.

They drove for about half an hour, and then the rental car swerved into the entrance of a private airstrip. Half a dozen small propeller planes were parked outside a lineup of sheds and a prefab terminal and control tower.

Meg could stay silent no longer. "We're flying somewhere?"

Harris did not answer.

Heart sinking, Aiden guessed at the latest catastrophe — separation. Meg on one plane, himself on another, flown to different prisons, hundreds, maybe thousands of miles apart. It would be the only blow they had not yet suffered — the final step in the dismantling of the Falconer family.

The agent removed the handcuffs that connected them to the car, but left them shackled together.

"We have the right to know what's going on!" Aiden insisted.

"What's going on is I need a cup of coffee. And you kids could probably use a snack. Come on. Out of the car."

The terminal had a lunch counter that overlooked

the runway. Harris ordered his usual extra-large coffee. Meg inhaled an enormous bowl of chicken noodle soup, managing it all left-handed.

Aiden refused to eat, although he was starving and exhausted from the five-hour work detail. "Why are we still handcuffed?" he snapped.

"You're kidding, right?" Harris swept him with a scornful glance. "Don't even go there."

Outside, the buzz of a propeller grew louder. Through the picture window, they watched a twin-engine plane touch down lightly, brake, and taxi toward the building.

Harris downed the rest of his coffee. "This is us." He led his prisoners out through the double doors. There they stood at the edge of the tarmac, watching as a ground attendant opened the plane's hatch and folded the stairway down.

Harris reached over and removed the shackles from each wrist.

Aiden stood poised, his heart pounding. This was the moment he'd been dreading.

If we were both going on that plane, he would have left the cuffs on!

His suspicions had been correct. He and his sister were about to be separated.

They couldn't let it happen. Not now, not *ever*.

They had no future, no family. All they had was each other.

He reached out and touched Meg's arm, trying to transmit a silent message: *Run!*

And then someone appeared in the doorway of the plane.

Aiden goggled, unable to believe his eyes. Surely he was hallucinating, driven to madness by crushing sorrow, paralyzing disappointment, and the relentless pressure of life on the run.

The passenger was Dr. John Falconer. His wife was right behind him.

Mom and Dad.

All at once, Meg was flying across the tarmac. Aiden watched as she hurled herself into her father's arms.

Harris gave Aiden a gentle shove from behind. "Well . . . go!"

Aiden stumbled forward, as if he had forgotten how to walk. The planet seemed to pitch beneath his feet. He might have fallen if not for his mother's frantic embrace.

"It's over, Aiden!" she murmured through tears of emotion. "My God, look how *tall* you are!"

It had been more than a year since the parents and their children had been together — a year of desperation, hopelessness, and misery. Now the shattered family clung together as if trying to fuse the pieces of their broken lives and make themselves whole.

Harris blew his nose with a loud honk and blinked eyes that were surprisingly moist. "We should probably find a TV. At six o'clock, the FBI is issuing a statement that John and Louise Falconer have been proven innocent by new evidence and have been released."

"Aiden!" Meg's eyes shone. "We did it!"

He was bewildered. "But we *didn't* do it! We *failed*!"

From his pocket, Harris produced a small tape recorder and pressed PLAY.

The audio transported Aiden and Meg instantly back to that terrifying night on the Turnbull farm. Even their parents recognized the chilling voice on the tape — the voice of their onetime friend Frank Lindenauer.

"*. . . Do you know how easy it was to sucker two college professors into working for HORUS? When I told them I was CIA, and they'd be helping their country, they were like puppy dogs, eager to do anything I asked. . . .*"

"But that's impossible!" Aiden breathed. "I never made that tape! I couldn't get to my recorder —"

Harris supplied the answer. "Your friend Mr. Turnbull — the one who's so handy with a shotgun — is in the middle of a lease dispute with his land- lord, one Elias Holyfield. Turns out Holyfield had the whole house bugged. This recording comes from his system."

Meg's eyes were like saucers. "You were right, Aiden! It worked out exactly the way you planned! Just like in Mac Mulvey!"

"*Mac Mulvey?*" John Falconer's jaw dropped. "*My* Mac Mulvey? From the books?"

"Oh, Dad!" Meg raved. "You wouldn't believe how many times something from Mac Mulvey saved our necks!"

Their father was horrified. "But I make all that up! I never meant for anybody to actually *do* it!"

Louise Falconer drew her children close. "I still can't get my mind around what you two went through for us. I can't imagine any other kids who would do it — or even try."

"Let's hope there aren't any," Harris put in feel- ingly. He turned to Aiden and Meg. "Not that you asked, but the charges against you have been dropped — every last one. You're welcome."

Aiden pressed his luck. "Agent Harris, what about Mr. Turnbull? He didn't mean to shoot you."

"He meant to shoot me. What saves him is he thought I was Lindenauer. He even gets to keep his farm. The judge ruled that Holyfield's surveillance was harassment." The FBI man grimaced. "Don't be so quick to send your former boss a congratulations card. You've got him to thank for your holiday at Danforth. I never would have let them send you to that chamber of horrors, but I was on the operating table at the time — having thirty pieces of buckshot picked out of my gut."

John Falconer addressed the despised agent who had arrested him and his wife a year and a half earlier and then hounded their children across the country.

"I guess we're never going to be friends," he said formally. "But you came through for us in the end. You'll never know how much it means to our family."

Harris, who could see exactly how much it meant to their family, had one more offer. "This plane is gassed up and ready to take you wherever you want to go. Maybe you should be on a beach for a couple of weeks while the country gets used to the fact that you're not the enemy anymore."

The four Falconers regarded one another blankly, weighing the suggestion. The parents had been locked up for so long that the idea of choice had become alien to them. And their kids had been fugitives, slaves to their quest and the urgent need to stay free and keep on running.

Finally, it was the youngest of them, Meg, who spoke for all.

"We've spent enough time away. There's only one place we want to go right now — "

When the grin split her face, it came with such intensity that it almost hurt. She wondered how long it had been since she'd last felt joy.

"Take us home."

KIDNAPPED

A THRILLING NEW TRILOGY

WITH MEG AND AIDEN FALCONER

BY

GORDON KORMAN

WHEN HIS SISTER MEG IS ABDUCTED
RIGHT IN FRONT OF HIS EYES, IT'S UP
TO AIDEN FALCONER, WITH THE HELP OF
FBI AGENT HARRIS, TO FIND HER—
WHILE THERE'S STILL TIME!

■SCHOLASTIC

www.scholastic.com

KIDNP